making a KILLING

Cori Nevruz

PRAISE FOR MAKING A KILLING

"Loved this book! Natalia was a very entertaining ... Villian? Hero? Victim? Still pondering! Great twist, too" – *Leslie B, Online Review*

"I really enjoyed this book... If you're looking for **a quick read that'll keep you turning pages**, I recommend Noxious for sure! It's an entertaining story and it'll keep you wondering what happens next. I especially enjoyed the flashbacks into Natalia's early life, she was a very well rounded character." —*Michaela B., thriller reader*

"An exciting and fascinating tale of family dynamics, corporate games manship... and murder. Lots of murder. I highly recommend buying this book and strapping yourself in for **a wild ride!**" —*J.T., Online Review*

"If you are a slow reader, you're going to need more time because **you won't be able to put it down!**" —*Early Reader Review*

"From the beginning of the book **I was on the edge of my seat** trying to figure out what Natalia would do next! You'll hate then love some of the characters and the whole time you try to guess what's next—but as the author does best—keeps surprising you up until the very last page! Mind blowing!" —*Ashley, Online Review*

"Brilliant, complex, edgy... a thriller through and through. The colorful characters and high stakes plot are full steam ahead the whole time.

The bottom line—read it. You won't be sorry and you won't be able to put it down." — *J. Leigh Jackson, Thriller Author*

"**I loved Natalia, Stuart & Bunny**! I couldn't help but relate and empathize with the "bad guys" of this thriller." – *Sharon C, Online Review*

"**This book was fantastic**. The writing is superb. The characters are intriguing and well written. The pacing is perfect, I was able to read this in one day. I ended up liking Natalia even though she's not really a very moral person. The ending had a huge twist that I did not see coming. I highly recommend this book and I am excited to see more from this author." – *Katy, ARC Reader*

contents

For my boys.
I will always be your biggest fan...
in a cow suit.

Excerpt from New World Business Journal

MBI: Desperate or Genius

Anna Miller

Against their conservative history, MBI made big moves this year by bringing on one of this generation's most well-known analytical minds, the creative yet unconventional Stuart Vladigan. Only time will tell whether the hire was pure desperation or sheer genius. After a half-century of leading the tech world, MBI recently reached a point where they would not survive in the new fast-paced world if they didn't make a significant change. The previously highly-touted company was on the brink of extinction and hemorrhaging money for nearly a decade.

With the hiring of Vladigan, the once powerful player in the technology sector MBI threw a Hail Mary in the final seconds of what appeared to be their last big game. Younger than any previous MBI Chief Executive Officer by at least twenty years, Vladigan's relative youth is overshadowed by his brilliant analytical mind, having been recognized by the masses as the most significant code writer of all time. However, unlike the previous leadership, Vladigan isn't afraid to ruffle feathers. His bold and sometimes brash personality may rub the good old boys the wrong way, but he is in a league of his own in the eyes of the up-and-coming techies. The mammoth-sized company, at nearly four hundred thousand employees, has not intimidated the new CEO in the least, as Vladigan did not hesitate to immediately lay off 20 percent of the MBI workforce while instituting a hiring freeze stating, "We need to learn how to work lean." In addition to the drastic cut in headcount, Vladigan mercilessly announced the phasing out of the company's longtime pension program stating, "We are the last dinosaur in the game. The bloated workforce and retirement payouts have to end."

Employees have long praised MBI for its benefits and hefty pension payouts to those who put in the time. What people had seen as their reward at the end of a long career, Vladigan viewed as "paying people not to work."

While MBI did show improvement in their first quarterly earnings with Vladigan at the helm, not losing money is simply not enough to keep MBI afloat. "Breaking even is not the goal of any business." As ruthless and unforgiving as Vladigan appears on paper, he has, so far, been fiscally correct.

Will wild card Stuart Vladigan be able to bring the company back to prominence, or will he be the man responsible for taking down the last of the dinosaurs?

THe ForBIDDen MIrror

Natalia stood buck-ass naked in front of the full-length mirror in her mother's dreary bedroom. The wall of open windows let in plenty of sunlight, but the dim lighting and the dark wood paneling on the walls gave the room the feel of a cave. Natalia loved the ornate mirror with its fine-grain mahogany wood and delicate detailing. Though her mother warned her countless times not to enter the room, Natalia liked to sneak a peek, always careful not to leave a trace. For as long as she could remember, every other mirror in the house had been removed or painted over with thick, black paint. "Not one thing about what you see in that mirror matters," her mother hissed when she caught Natalia gazing at her own reflection. She kicked Natalia out of the room and slammed the door behind her, yelling, "That mirror is flattering, but the reflection is not reality. You may look normal, but you are not!"

Standing completely still, she stared at her long, dirty-blonde hair hanging over her perfect, perky breasts. Her eyes wandered to admire her slim figure, her blemish-free, pale skin, and finally, her face. Her lips were full without being oversized. Her cheekbones were defined but not so sharp as to make the rest of her face look caved in. Some would say her nose was large for her face, but she thought it fit her perfectly. Her eyes were like large green olives with giant, black pits. Her right eye had a small, brown birthmark on the green iris, like a satellite orbiting a sizeable black moon.

Natalia lost track of how long she had been standing in front of the mirror. She wanted to absorb every detail, every curve, everything she had been deprived of all these years. Her mother always told her she was "weird," "strange," and "not suited for society," but as Natalia looked at her reflection, she didn't see what was so unusual. Her dear mother no longer let her go out in public because she was different from others, and they were frightened of her. She said they would be mean to her. She told her that they would be cruel. Over and over, she would stress that Natalia couldn't handle it. But, when she reflected on the so-called "cruel world," Natalia couldn't imagine anyone who could be meaner or crueler than her mother.

The pungent smell of cinnamon wafted in on a breeze through the open window. When Natalia turned to look, she saw a pretty, red Cardinal sitting on the windowsill. The color red always smelled like cinnamon—even blood. Strangely enough, death itself had no smell at all.

She turned back to the forbidden mirror, admiring her reflection one last time, then glanced over the shoulder of her reflection to see her mother's dead, rotting corpse on the bed.

HOW TO MAKE A KILLING

Stuart Vladigan sat on his one-of-a-kind, crocodile skin sectional, hunched over his oversized marble coffee table, poring over a pile of documents. The last of the remaining daylight shining through the penthouse floor-to-ceiling windows only enhanced the ambiance of his elegant living room. With instrumental, downtempo music playing through the speakers hidden in the walls, fragrant candles burning, and his wife, Bunny, sitting in her overstuffed, fluffy chair filing her nails between audible sips of her margarita, it was a miracle he could concentrate at all.

Stuart wasn't what one would call a typical white-collar executive. He worked, lived, played, and loved differently than anyone else. He was brash, had a keen eye for business, and had never been afraid to swim against the current. He cared little about what others thought of him but clung faithfully to those who understood him. Bunny, for example, was a centerfold model a decade ago. She didn't mind that he worked long hours, sometimes leaving town on business. He didn't mind that she spent most of her time at the spa, shopping, or the gym with her personal trainer. For the most part, their relationship was past the point of steamy romance, but they both appreciated their ability to sit in silence together, taking in the opulent life they worked so hard to earn. He respected and admired her, as Bunny did him, and that seemed to be all they needed to hold their marriage together.

Bunny stuck her fluffy-slippered foot out over the coffee table and nudged Stuart's martini glass closer to him.

He dropped his papers with a sigh and muttered, "Why did I take over a company that was ever in the pension game? I immediately cut the pension program to all new employees and bought out as many existing enrollees as possible. But for the retirees and current employees who refused the buyout, I have to pay all these geezers millions of dollars to golf or sit on their asses feeding breadcrumbs to pigeons in the park." He patted Bunny's slippered foot, picked up his glass, and took a long sip, finishing his drink.

"What's worse is that MBI's pension program states that if the pension holder dies, the financial benefit is passed on to their spouse. The benefactor and the spouse need to expire before the enormous recurring company cost can be unburdened. It's a fucking money pit. We could be making a killing without these pension payouts. I mean, how long are these guys going to live? Fortunately, Johnson will be retiring next week. He is such a good ole boy, so obviously, we don't see eye-to-eye. In reality he's being forced out rather than retiring, but I'll let him leave with some dignity." Stuart looked off into the distance at nothing in particular, deep in thought. "I'll bring in my own CFO who will understand my financial vision."

As if abruptly brought back to reality, he said, "Oh shit, I can't imagine how much we will have to pay out to Johnson. He has probably been working at MBI since the fifties." Stuart looked over to see if Bunny was laughing with him and noticed she wasn't even paying attention. She was wearing her wireless headphones and watching her favorite reality show on her phone while filing her already perfectly manicured nails.

Stuart glanced over her shoulder to see one of Bunny's old framed magazine covers hanging on the wall beside his huge pink "YOU DO YOU" neon sign. This had become Stuart's mantra over the years. He was known to march to the beat of a different drum and tried to encourage others to do the same. Don't follow the crowd, do your own thing. If he were to succeed or even fail, it would be with his ideas and actions, not someone else's. It isn't easy working your way up the corporate ladder without kissing a lot of asses as you climb. Still, his renegade personality earned him notoriety in the business world. He turned around three reputable companies before recently joining MBI as their Chief Executive Officer.

Bunny must have felt the weight of his stare. She glanced in his direction and saw that he was looking over her shoulder. She paused her show and pulled her headphones down around her neck.

"You okay?" she asked.

"Yeah. I'm just thinking about this talk I'll give at a technology conference tomorrow. The Board of Directors wants me to take the opportunity to discuss some of our proven technology to squash concerns about potential revenue dips. Of course, I want to do my normal thing that people come out to see... you know, me, my vision of the new software in the pipeline... plus a lot of off-the-cuff jokes. I didn't get this far by being a walking commercial, did I?"

"You do you, sweet thang," Bunny said sweetly in her light southern accent she had worked so hard to hide.

Stuart rolled his eyes. "You do know that it is totally against all rules of social etiquette to use someone else's catchphrase to them, right?" he said, slightly joking.

Bunny stood, seductively bent over to pick her empty glass up, then looked Stuart in the eyes. She smiled and began to make her way out of the room in a slow saunter.

"Hey," Stuart called after her, mesmerized by the rhythmic sway of her ass. "You didn't tell me what you think I should do tomorrow."

She stopped in her tracks without turning around and nonchalantly pointed to the "YOU DO YOU" sign she was passing by.

THE SECRET'S OUT

Natalia sat at a small, well-worn table next to the large, plate-glass window at a corner cafe. She picked at the cracked varnish and stared out the window thinking back to the events from a week ago when she sat with her mother at a table just like this.

After a typical morning of her mother's insults: *Why can't you be normal? It's because of you that I'm cooped up in here... I will never find another man with you around... Odd. You are odd. ... Stop looking at me... I don't care what you smell...* Natalia sat at the table, waiting for her mother to join her for lunch.

When her mother finally arrived, Natalia knew something was different. The tangy, sour smell of garbage typically followed her mother, but her scent that day was the strong and shocking smell of black pepper. Was that a smile on her mother's face? That couldn't be the smell of joy. The sharp smell, accompanied by a smile, brought only one thought to Natalia's mind: evil. She had never seen such a disgusting look before. She sighed and averted her eyes toward the ceiling, thankful her mother didn't smile often.

Thinking back on the uncomfortable conversation and her mother's shit-eating grin caused goosebumps to cover Natalia's arms. She shivered and glanced up at the ceiling, looking for a fan or a vent, fully aware that it wasn't a breeze that gave her the chills. Her mother confessed to her a secret she had kept from her daughter her entire life. How would Natalia's life have been different without secrets, lies, and deception?

She may never know, but today she planned to change her life for good.

NOT COUSINS

Daniel Webber walked into his neighborhood coffee shop, set down his laptop and briefcase at his favorite table, and made his way to the counter.

"Good morning, Daniel. The usual?" asked the flirty barista, batting her glued-on eyelashes rapidly in his direction.

"I'm great. Thanks, Patty. And you?" He was never very smooth with social banter and often made the mistake of anticipating what other people would say incorrectly. "I mean. Sure. Yes. Thank you. The usual." He blushed and looked down at his feet.

"Go ahead and take a seat. I'll bring it right out," she said with a wink that made his cheeks burn pink.

Women hit on him all the time, but he never got used to it. He supposed he was attractive enough at an average height, a stylish but professional length of dirty blonde hair, green eyes, and what women have said were movie-star-like, perfect teeth. He was fit and confident without being cocky, and this morning, he was wearing a custom-tailored suit, apparently an aphrodisiac to the ladies.

He settled down at the table, opened his laptop, and noticed another woman staring at him from a table by the window while waiting for his login screen to appear. She was wearing dark sunglasses, so he was not entirely sure she was staring, but it seemed like it.

He smiled at her; she smiled back, then he looked back at his computer.

Wow, this suit is a game changer, he thought to himself.

Without warning, the woman by the window jumped up and, with cat-like quickness and agility, ripped off her sunglasses, moved to his table, and plopped down right into the seat across from him. She looked about his age, somewhere in her mid to late twenties, but her movements and the way she carried herself made her seem younger. She wore an oversized, puffy, white blouse and contrasting rugged overalls. Her hair was pulled up in a ponytail, and she wore very little or no makeup.

She stared at him across the table with bright green eyes and a huge smile.

"Hi," Daniel said hesitantly, feeling quite confused.

"Hi," she said back quickly, still smiling as if she was holding in a juicy secret.

Before he could say anything else, the barista appeared over his guest's shoulder, placing a giant cinnamon roll and hot chocolate in front of her and his cappuccino in front of him. The waitress looked back and forth between the two, and a reluctant, maybe even jealous, half-smile appeared on her lips as she turned to head back to the counter.

The woman, now seated across from him, bit into her cinnamon roll, closed her eyes, and chewed, softly moaning as her jaw worked her pastry in slow motion.

"Good, huh?" Daniel said, not entirely understanding what was happening and wondering if someone was playing a trick on him or observing him as part of an odd social experiment. He took a minute to scan the cafe for onlookers, but the other patrons were in their own world.

With a big part of the cinnamon roll still in her mouth, she said, "My mom never let me have sweets," moaning again as she took a large sip of the steaming hot chocolate, her eyes rolling back in her head.

"So," Daniel started, hoping to find out what this woman wanted, "thanks for joining me, but I am preparing for a big conference today. My entire career depends on it. So, if you'll excuse me..."

"I wasn't sure how to approach you, so I thought I would go with surprise," she interrupted, not even registering what he had just said. She paused, and when he didn't say anything, she yelled, "SURPRISE! I'M YOUR SISTER!"

"That's a new one," he whispered, wondering if that was a pickup line.

Daniel blushed as he felt the weight of every other previously occupied customer's eyes on him while the girl or woman sitting across from him looked as though she didn't even notice or care that anyone else was in the cafe with them.

"Well, half-sister, I guess. My mother was our dad's mistress," she said matter-of-factly. She took another bite of the roll, moaned audibly, then with a full mouth mumbled, "For years and years and years." Her hands miming the passage of time by flipping through the air while she chewed.

"I didn't even know you existed until my mom told me last week. She wasn't allowed to say anything until after your mom died. Something to do with a restraining order... my mom said your mom was a real bitch." She took another sip from her mug, then stopped abruptly. "Oh, sorry about your mom, by the way. Tragic." She looked down at the table, shaking her head slowly. "My mom is dead, too," she said casually, as if comparing the color of their shirts.

She finally noticed the stunned look on his face and followed up with, "Don't worry, my mom was a bitch, too."

She laughed, wiped her hands thoroughly on her overalls, stood up, and locked eyes with Daniel holding out her right hand. "I am Natalia Zapakh. It is nice to meet you finally."

"Natalia?" Daniel questioned as if searching for an old memory, staring off to the left out of the cafe window.

"Yeeesssss," she sang playfully to him, batting her eyelashes.

"Oh. Yes. My dad, I mean, our dad, used to talk about you," Daniel muttered as he started connecting pieces of the puzzle that he didn't even know existed.

Natalia's cheery expression turned ice cold as her smile dropped. The eyes that moments ago were the same green shade as his turned dark. "You mean... you knew about me?" she said through clenched teeth.

"No, not really. Dad would sometimes extend business trips to visit his cousin, Tatiana. He told me that Tatiana had a daughter named Natalia." Daniel paused. "So, you're *that* Natalia. I guess then Tatiana wasn't his cousin?"

Her happy-go-lucky expression returned. She looked over both of her shoulders as if concerned someone would hear her, then with a wink, whispered with her hand up to her mouth, shielding her lips from pretend prying eyes, "Definitely not his cousin." She then let out a loud one-syllable laugh, again drawing the attention of the entire cafe.

Daniel was shocked at her outburst, but quickly regained his composure, glancing down at his watch. "Look, Natalia, I am thrilled to meet you. Shocked but thrilled. But I have a very important conference I am heading to this morning, and I need to finish preparing. I'm not exaggerating when

I tell you my livelihood, my future, my entire career, ride on what happens today."

If this woman was his half-sister, and he couldn't imagine why anyone would make up such a story, this was both a miracle and a blessing. He had so many questions for her. He wanted to learn everything there was to know about her. He had been an only child his entire life, and now, without warning, he wasn't. He wanted to stare at her longer to see what features they shared or see if she was anything like his dad. But no, he couldn't do this now. He had to prepare for the conference. If he had a half-sister, it would be more important than ever before that he gets back on his feet.

Daniel reached into his coat pocket, pulled out a business card, and started to write on the back. "Can you meet me at my place tonight? We can catch up then and get to know each other a bit. The address is on the back. It's only a few blocks from here."

Natalia looked at the card as if it were a precious childhood toy. She carefully pocketed the card in the bib's large, solo front pocket on her overalls and smiled.

After ten long and extremely uncomfortable seconds of her staring at him, Natalia stood up abruptly, walked around the table, and pulled Daniel up to stand. She wrapped her arms around him in a tight bear hug laying her head against his chest. He could see Patty, the barista, over Natalia's shoulder, eyeing them with evident curiosity. When Natalia broke their embrace, she gave him a two-fisted cheek squeeze as one would expect from their Great Aunt Gertrude, then turned to leave.

He rubbed his face as he watched her walk away, laughing rather loudly and muttering about cousins.

An Odd Place to Meet

Daniel had been planning for the conference for weeks. He previously worked as the Chief Financial Officer for three startups, all of which went under. Each experience taught him quite a lot, and the businesses only remained intact as long as they did due to his decisions, leadership, budgeting, and accounting. However, when the last three companies you worked for no longer existed, it looks like a big stain on your resume. He made good money, but he also spent good money. When his last company closed eight months ago, he set his sights on a more significant and stable company.

MBI, a household name in technology companies, had been around Daniel's entire life, specializing in computer systems, software, and networking. MBI's CFO announced a few weeks ago that he planned to retire at the end of this quarter. The MBI Chief Executive Officer, Stuart Vladigan, was seen as a bit of a rogue player who became wildly successful by bucking the system. Hiring Vladigan was the first move in MBI's history that went against their straitlaced, conservative roots. MBI needed to move away from traditional ways to right its financial ship and survive.

Vladigan was their answer. Indeed, when it came time to fill the vacant CFO role, he would want to hire someone young and hip rather than someone recommended by the board. Mr. Vladigan was scheduled to speak at the technology conference today, and Daniel saw this as his prime opportunity to meet and impress the CEO. Daniel needed the "chance encounter" now more than ever. His six-month severance package ended months ago, and his savings were dwindling. He never appreciated how much money his past companies spent on conference registrations until he had to pay out of pocket. His expense report and company credit card were sorely missed. He planned to arrive early and get front-row seats for when Mr. Vladigan spoke and ask a few scripted questions if the opportunity presented itself. Finally, he would introduce himself with a resume in hand at the meet and greet for which he had paid extra.

Unfortunately, all his planning hadn't paid off. Everything was working against him. He arrived an hour early to the presentation to ensure a good seat, but the first five rows were roped off, marked as reserved, and the next ten rows were already full. There were more early birds than worms. Beyond frustrated, Daniel listened as a conference representative took the stage to announce that there would be no questions and that the meet and greet had been canceled due to unforeseen circumstances. Partial refunds were forthcoming.

Disappointed, Daniel strategically placed himself behind a very petite Asian woman to ensure he could see the CEO and be seen. But, when all the seats were full and the presentation was about to start, the tiny woman switched places with the giant of a man seated next to her. Daniel could not see anything other than the back of his large head. Then, on top of it all, Mr. Vladigan spoke for less than ten minutes. Not that it mattered to Daniel; he wasn't there to listen, he was there to meet the man, and sadly, that appeared to be off the table.

As everyone cleared out of the large room, Daniel walked, with his head down, discouraged, to the conference's main room, where the technology firms and service providers were breaking down their booths. Rather than follow the massive crowd to the exit, he detoured to the bathroom. As he rounded the corner, he saw a man dressed in all black guarding the bathroom door. The guy reminded Daniel of an old-school prize fighter. He was not young, not super large, but you knew he was a dude who was not to be messed with. Those wrinkles on his face were likely from years of kicking ass. Daniel walked toward the bathroom and muttered, "I need to use the restroom."

The boxer look-alike nodded, and Daniel let himself in. He placed his briefcase on a shelf by the sink and walked over to the urinal, trying to calculate whether he had enough money to pay rent the next month. He thought he would receive at least a little money from his mother's estate, but she left everything to a tribe of Aborigines in Australia. He shouldn't have been surprised. She had always been selfish to the point that if she couldn't have it, no one would. If she was going to die, then everyone should be miserable. If she couldn't have the money, neither could he. He rolled his eyes, thinking about how much he hated her and missed her simultaneously, but also agreeing with Natalia's sentiment from earlier... she was a bitch. He laughed to himself, which caught the man's attention at the far urinal.

"I hope it's your dick you're laughing at, not mine," said the man as he turned around to wash his hands at the sink.

Daniel turned as he zipped, and to his surprise, he was mere feet away from Mr. Stuart Vladigan, the very man he came to see. This was the break he had been waiting for.

"Mr. Vladigan. Hi. Oh, of course, I wasn't laughing at you. I just remembered something from earlier."

"Well, that's reassuring, as long as you're not referring to my speech," Vladigan said with a smirk.

"I came here today to meet you." Daniel grabbed his briefcase from the shelf and hurried over to the counter as he dug through his briefcase to grab an envelope. "I would like to throw my hat in the ring for the CFO position at MBI. Enclosed is my resume. I think you will find that I am just what MBI needs," he said, a bit too robotic while handing over the envelope.

"This is exactly how I always imagined meeting my new CFO... in the men's room," Vladigan said with a laugh.

Daniel smiled uncomfortably and wiped his sweaty palms on his pants, trying to remember if he had even washed his hands. "Thanks you for your time. It nice to meet you," Daniel mumbled awkwardly before quickly exiting the bathroom, not entirely sure what he just said, but knowing that it was not even close to what he had scripted in the coffee shop earlier. He walked away at a pace so fast that he was gliding like a competitive speed walker with that awkward hip rock keeping at least one foot touching the ground at all times. He slowed down, thinking about his luck, then stopped, realizing he had never introduced himself. He grabbed a business card from his coat pocket, currently affiliated with no company, and returned to the bathroom. He saw Mr. Vladigan and what he can only assume now was his bodyguard walking toward him, laughing hysterically.

"Oh, speak of the devil," Vladigan said, elbowing his protector.

"I realized I never introduced myself. I guess the bathroom isn't the right place to shake hands anyway. My name is Daniel Webber. Here is my card. I look forward to hearing from you soon."

Without waiting for an answer, nod, or any acknowledgment, he turned and, as quickly as he could, put distance between himself, the conference, the building, and, more importantly, the CEO.

GETTING TO KNOW YOU

Natalia could hear Daniel outside the door, fumbling with his keys. She hadn't expected him yet, but she was ready enough. She snatched the master key from the countertop that she had lifted off the housekeeper earlier and shoved it into her pocket just as the door opened. Daniel looked shocked and confused to see her standing in his kitchen, but his expression soon changed to one more pleasantly surprised when he saw that she had set up a huge spread of appetizers and was walking toward him with cocktails.

"I thought I would come early and surprise you after your big day. I hope you don't mind," she said, flashing her large, puppy dog eyes, trying to look as innocent and sincere as possible.

"Well, this isn't exactly what I had in mind when I asked you to meet me here, but I am glad to see you. I called the doorman on my way to the conference to tell him I was expecting you this evening, so I am glad he let you in."

The key in her pocket felt like it was burning a hole through her overalls, taunting her to tell him that she actually posed as a housekeeper for over an hour to get into his apartment. But, seeing that he made his own assumptions, she decided to let him believe what he wanted. Not saying anything was not lying after all, right?

"Where did you order all of this food from? I need their number. It looks amazing," Daniel said, taking in the charcuterie board featuring five different types of cheese, artisan crackers, black olives stuffed with blue cheese, red grapes, thinly sliced meats, and crispy breadsticks.

Natalia bent over behind the counter to pull a tray of bacon-wrapped dates and crusty bread topped with fig jam and goat cheese out of the oven.

"Actually," she said, placing the pan on the stovetop and decorating a platter with warm appetizers. "I made it all."

"How do you know how to do this? This spread is incredible," he said, popping an olive in his mouth.

"I watch a lot of videos," she said from behind her glass as she sipped. She wanted to elaborate and let him know that almost everything she knew came from the internet, thanks to her soul-crushing and sheltering mother, but she was trying to hide anything from him that would be deemed abnormal for a city-dwelling adult. She certainly didn't want to let him know that she had not yet found a place to stay in the city. In fact, after meeting him at the coffee shop, she wandered the city, taking in the new smells. That was until she came up with the idea of playing maid and trying her skills at pickpocketing.

Daniel picked up a bacon-wrapped date, examined it, shook his head in disbelief, and said, "Well, I'm floored. I needed this today. My plan for meeting the head honcho didn't work out quite how I had hoped." He went on to explain the events of the conference and how he ended up cornering the prospective boss of his dream company in the bathroom.

Natalia laughed at his story and then peppered him with questions about that job specifically, as well as his current lack of one. He told her he was pretty much broke and didn't have enough money to pay rent. At first, she couldn't believe that someone who had been so successful and climbed the corporate ladder could have no money, but then she looked around his small yet immaculately decorated apartment and realized where his money had gone. Not only did every furnishing look expensive, but his apartment was located in a desirable location on one of the top floors of a doorman building.

"I have money, Daniel. I could move in with you, stay on your couch, and pay your rent until you get back on your feet." With just a crack in the preverbal door, Natalia barged right through in hopes of solving her current homeless state.

She could see that her offer touched him deeply but that his pride would not allow it, which was unfortunate because she did need a place to stay. "Thank you, Natalia. You're very kind, but I can't accept. I need to handle this on my own. I'll try even harder to find a job, and when I finally land the right one, you and I can spend more time together and get to know each other."

Natalia wondered if Daniel meant that without a job, she couldn't be part of his life. It didn't make sense. Why didn't he take her up on her offer? Then, the two of them could be a family.

"I put all of my eggs in one basket with MBI. There were dozens of other important industry contacts I could've met today. I could've networked with other companies, but I had my sights set on the golden egg and blew it."

"Too bad it all ended so early," Natalia sighed, sipping her drink and leaning against the wall.

Daniel perked up. "That's it! There is a conference after-party of sorts at a new club tonight. We can go, have a good time, and maybe get lucky and meet some bigwigs."

"We?" Natalia asked, trying not to get her hopes up in case she misheard.

"Yes. Come with me, Natalia. It'll be fun. We may have to wait a while to get in, but with my conference ticket, admission is free. What do you say?"

Natalia downed her nearly full drink, walked around the kitchen counter, kissed Daniel on the cheek, grabbed her bag, and ran to the bathroom to change, calling out behind her, "Just give me twenty."

***

Daniel changed clothes into something more suited to club attire but kept it professional, remembering the purpose of the outing. He reapplied deodorant, added some cologne, and then walked back to the kitchen to have more of the delectable goodies his half-sister had made.

"Half-sister," he said aloud while shaking his head. How had he gone his whole life not knowing he had a half-sister? Or, more accurately, her entire life...

He recalled times when his dad would take trips to see his so-called cousin. His mother would pout all weekend and never once told him why. He shook the thought out of his mind, flopped onto the couch, and turned on the TV.

"...who allegedly took a bag of fast food as payment from one neighbor to murder his other neighbor's dog." The basic, non-accented voice came from the news, flashing a picture of a random drive-through restaurant on the screen.

"What the hell is wrong with people?" Daniel mainly muttered to himself but also to Natalia, who was reentering the room behind him.

He turned in her direction, having more to say about the absurd news story, but was instantly distracted. Gone was his innocent half-sister in overalls and pigtails from mere moments ago. The woman that walked out of his hallway bathroom looked like a sophisticated supermodel. Her hair was down, hanging in loose curls over her shoulders. She donned a sparkly, sequined cocktail dress cut low in the front and high on the legs. She was also much taller now in her stilettos. Where earlier, her face had been bare, there were now bright, red lips, black, lined eyes, and glitter on her eyelids. She looked classy, not overdone.

"Wow, Natalia. You look great. Most women take hours to get ready. You pulled a full 180 and aged ten years in less than..." He paused, looking down at his watch, then continued, "Fifteen minutes."

Daniel turned off the TV, stood, brushed wrinkles from his pants, then walked over to Natalia. He held out his elbow for her to take hold, grabbed a roadie cocktail, and headed out to schmooze.

Party in the Club

In the hired car, Natalia felt normal. She felt wanted. Today she was not just a sheltered outcast. Natalia was beaming from her big brother's compliments. It made her happy to see him happy. He looked proud to have her on his arm. He seemed impressed with her cooking and serving. After seeing his reaction to the news, however, she now knew he wouldn't be happy with things she had done in her past with animals, not to mention humans.

It had started to drizzle, but not even the crappy weather could dampen Daniel's positive attitude. She watched the rain through the window and thought about her little experiments—just last week, she spent the afternoon standing in the rain at a bus stop observing people. She wanted to see how many people would leave their drinks unattended in a public place absentmindedly. She punished those who were too engrossed in their devices to pay attention with several squirts of eye drops into their unsupervised drinks. She didn't think she used enough to kill anyone but didn't take the time to find out. She assumed her victims went home with painful stomach cramps and explosive diarrhea. She enjoyed people-watching but loved being karma's little helper even more. And she would do it all for free. She didn't even need a bag of burgers.

She smiled while staring out the rain-streaked window at the bright lights streaming by like watercolor finger paintings. She caught a glimpse of her reflection and inwardly thanked the internet for the makeup tutorial and the random lady on the third floor whose room she had "cleaned" earlier for the dress and makeup. *More like cleaned out*, she laughed to herself.

When they arrived at the club, Daniel dropped his head and walked like a dejected pouty-faced teen to the end of the long line queuing up. Natalia grabbed his hand and walked past at least forty people in line to the bouncer at the front. He nodded at her and unhooked the red velvet rope allowing them access.

Daniel stared at her in awe, and when they were a safe distance from the door, she answered the question written all over his face, "Internet videos. They say that people rarely question you if you act like you belong. It's all about confidence, Daniel."

The club was dark, with blinking strobe lights, disco balls, and small neon blinkers accenting the tables and walls. Cages anchored the four corners of the large room, each containing a woman on exhibit in glowing neon bikini bottoms. Their breasts were bare, but each nipple was painted in glow-in-the-dark paint. Natalia squinted at the caged woman nearest her to see if the nipple coverings were stickers but couldn't tell without getting closer. The loud music thumped with such intensity that she could feel the beat through the souls of her shoes. If there were words to the song playing, she couldn't hear them over the dominant bass line. The smoke machines fogged up the dance floor, personifying the air as it bounced with the music. Natalia closed her eyes and inhaled deeply, absorbing the smell she would associate with this club. With one sense tuned out, she could detect the smell of an electrical fire under the stink of sweat and whatever sticky stuff she was standing in. Opening her eyes, she glanced around, moving two feet this way and four feet that way. She noticed the electrical smell grew stronger the closer she got to a couple making out on a sofa. Attraction smells like electrical fire. That is a great one for her to remember.

Daniel caught her eye as he awkwardly bounced between gyrating bodies, spilling some of the drinks he was holding on unsuspecting partiers. When Natalia set eyes on the two large cocktails, her mouth fell open.

"Did you buy those?" she asked.

"Of course. How else would we get drinks?" Daniel answered.

Natalia stared at him down her nose in disappointment. When he didn't understand her frustration, she threw her arms to the side and spun in a slow-motion circle as if she was modeling her outfit. He gasped, "Why on earth would I exploit my half-sister? You don't have to 'WORK' for your drinks," he said, throwing up finger quotes and spilling a little more.

"You're the broke one. I'm just saying..." she trailed off, taking a long sip of her drink, which was tall and delicious but clearly with very little alcohol.

Head nodding to the beat, Natalia watched Daniel take in his surroundings. His eyes drifted toward a bachelorette party in a roped-off area across the dance floor. She thought of reminding him to look for his business contacts but didn't dare assume that one of the women in the group couldn't be one of them.

"Oh my gosh, Natalia!" he screamed with the excitement of a ten-year-old girl getting a pony. "Do you know who is over there in the VIP section?" Daniel said loudly into her ear so she could hear him over the music.

She stared at him, eyes wide, while taking another sip from her drink, waiting for him to tell her already.

"That's the guy I was telling you about. Stuart Vladigan. The CEO I spoke with about the job. Do you think he will remember me if I talk to him now?"

She paused in disbelief before leaning over and speaking loudly, "You're asking me if I think the guy you cornered in the bathroom today with his dick in his hand will remember you?" Natalia asked, deadpan. "Yeah, I think he'll remember you."

"Let's go. What do I have to lose?" Daniel said excitedly and made his way through the crowd, pulling a very hesitant Natalia behind him.

When they approached the VIP section, the bouncer, who looked more like an professional linebacker, kept his arms crossed in front of him and shook his head, daring them to move closer. Natalia was unsure how he even saw them standing there with the dark sunglasses he wore in the already dark club.

"Hey, brother-man. What do I need to do to get in there? I need to talk to Stuart. He knows me," Daniel said, coming across as less confident and more try-hard.

Natalia rolled her eyes behind him, quite sure his begging and attempt at camaraderie with the bouncer would not get them access. She glanced up at the plush couch where Mr. Vladigan was sitting only a few tables over from the bachelorette party and caught the eye of a woman sitting next to him. The woman was beautiful, older than Natalia, maybe approaching forty. Her long, platinum blonde hair looked freshly brushed with not a hair out of place. Her bright blue eyes lined in black eyeliner and surrounded by long, flirty eyelashes were mesmerizing even from a distance. Natalia watched as the woman leaned over and whispered in the drunk CEO's ear. The man looked at Natalia, obviously intrigued, then when he looked over at Daniel, it was clear he recognized him. He called out to the bouncer and enthusiastically waved Natalia and Daniel through. Daniel ran up the short staircase like a kid racing to be the first to sit on Santa's lap. The closer they got to the Vladigan VIP table, the more Natalia could smell pepper. Not the vegetable pepper, but the spice that, when inhaled, makes people sneeze. That smell was an unfortunate reminder of her childhood, making her stomach turn.

"Mr. Vladigan, it's nice to see you again. I am not sure if you remember, but—" Daniel shouted over the music, slightly out of breath, as the two walked up to the seating area.

Daniel stopped when he was interrupted by none other than the man he was excited to see.

"Bunny, Francisco, you guys need to hear this. Blaine, Seth, Rodney, come over here a minute," he called out to some associates at the next table.

"This guy…" Vladigan paused, closing his eyes to a squint while searching his memory for the name.

"Daniel," Daniel said, kindly reminding him.

"This guy, Daniel, gave me his resume in the bathroom today at the conference. Can you imagine how desperate you have to be to approach someone in the bathroom?" he said, laughing with his buddies. The woman and man at his table, whom Natalia assumed were Bunny and Francisco, just stared and did not look amused.

"Do you think he saw the size of my dick and, at that moment, knew he had to work for me?" Stuart ribbed more.

Bunny and Francisco rolled their eyes at Stuart, clearly not finding Stuart's childlike bullying entertaining. Natalia locked eyes with Francisco, and the overpowering smell of electrical fire returned, but this time she felt a jolt similar to a static shock. Natalia was jostled forward as a couple locking lips in the VIP section bumped aggressively into her. When Stuart spoke again, she thought about slicing one of their legs open with her stilettos.

"Do you guys think I should give him a shot?" Stuart asked even louder. He paused, looking for feedback, then threw back the shot of tequila in front of him, laughing so hard that most of it squirted out of his nose.

Daniel's face was bright red at this point. He was humiliated, but to his credit, he didn't throw insults back or run to escape the situation.

"Too late!" Stuart said with a fake sad face, tracing an invisible tear track down his cheek with his middle finger. "I tossed his resume in the bin before the door to the bathroom closed behind him." Though Bunny and Francisco looked bored and not the slightest bit amused, this made Stuart's ass-kissing co-workers at the other table laugh even louder.

Natalia was glaring at the cruel man, feeling a burning in her chest. Her anger grew with each condescending remark that so easily poured out of his mouth.

Daniel didn't drop his head and sulk; he looked the man in the eyes and calmly said, "Thank you for your time, Mr. Vladigan." He turned and walked out of the VIP section toward the bar.

***

Hurtful memories of Natalia's childhood surfaced. Suddenly, she was back in grade school playing Good Morning, Mr. Judge with classmates. In the game, one player would sit in a chair facing the wall. The other kids in the classroom would walk up, one at a time, behind the person in the chair and say, "Good Morning, Mr. Judge." Most everyone changed their voice to something very high and squeaky or very low and deep. The person in the chair then had to guess who it was. If they were right, the speaker would become "it" and take over as the guesser. If they were wrong, the guesser stayed in the seat and waited for the next speaker to approach.

One memorable day in fifth grade, Bella, the bleeder, got yet another bloody nose in the middle of class. Mrs. Garriss had to run her out to the school nurse and told the class to play a "nice and quiet game of Good Morning, Mr. Judge" until she returned. Natalia wasn't friends with anyone in the class, so they picked her, knowing she wouldn't know anyone's voice.

Natalia sat on the hard plastic chair which chilled the back of her bare legs, facing the wall with her feet crossed at the ankles and her hands clasped on her lap. She closed her eyes and tried only to use her nose to smell when someone approached her chair.

The first classmate approached and spoke in a distinctly fake, low-pitched voice in a slow lisp, "Good Morning, Mr. Judge."

"Jackson. Pine trees and pepper," Natalia said.

The class was quiet behind her for an unbearably long time before someone in the back of the class yelled angrily, "No. You're wrong."

Natalia kept her eyes closed, waiting for the next student to approach. She heard the soft tap of sneakers, followed by a little giggle. A monotone, robot-mocking voice came, "Good Morning, Mr. Judge."

"Sally. Pomegranate."

There was a gasp from the back of the room, followed by another voice saying, "Wrong, again."

She knew she wasn't wrong. Each kid in class had their own smell, but the bullies also had the irritating odor of pepper. Before the next person even stepped up to the back of her chair, she said, "Michael. Rotten fish and pepper."

Michael grabbed her chair, yelling, "What did you call me!"

But right as he did, Mrs. Garriss walked back into the room.

"Michael. Take your seat!" Mrs. Garriss snapped. "This doesn't look like the nice, calm game I asked for. I am very disappointed." As arguments from the classroom erupted about how Natalia cheated, Mrs. Garriss looked at her sympathetically, smelling of sweet perfume.

"You may also take your seat, dear," she said.

Natalia stood, straightened her dress, and, while walking back to her seat, said, "I won. They cheated, but I still won."

They didn't understand how she was winning, but they also couldn't prove how she was cheating. They hated her and turned her gift against her at every possible opportunity. They would bring it up as if it was something to be proud of, only to mock her and occasionally send Natalia into an embarrassing sneezing fit as she inhaled their peppery meanness.

***

The booming bass brought Natalia back to the present, standing in the club, staring at yet another bully. She stood there, frozen, wanting to hurt the man who hurt her big brother. Bunny locked eyes with her and gave her a sympathetic, almost apologetic look. Stuart stood and announced to anyone listening, "I need to piss." He stood, stretched, and stumbled down the three stairs out of the VIP section.

Natalia left as well, watching and following him as he made his way through the crowd. After dancing for a few seconds with a costumed stranger and taking a sip of some dude's beer, Stuart walked into the men's room. No sooner had the door shut behind him had Natalia entered. She stood with her back against the door and watched as he stood at the urinal. When he shook, zipped, and turned around, he was startled to see her standing there.

"Well, hello," he said seductively, walking to the wall of sinks, "You and your boyfriend have a thing about confronting people in bathrooms, don't you?"

She calmly walked up to him. She was only an inch shorter than him in her high heels, so they were close to being eye-to-eye.

"Daniel is my big brother," she said matter-of-factly, slightly emphasizing Daniel's name, unable to believe he had forgotten it again already.

"Whatever, girl. You do you."

"You do you? What the hell does that mean? Is that some sort of masturbation reference?" she quipped.

"What? No!" Stuart said defensively. "That's my saying. You know, my catchphrase. Do you even know who I am?"

"Yes. Of course I do. You are the asshole who insulted my big brother in front of all those people." Natalia drew out the word "all" while gesturing out toward the non-bathroom part of the club. "I am not worldly or well-traveled, but I have spent the last ten years researching the most effective way to kill without leaving a trace. I have things that piss me off. These pet peeves, so to speak, get me so worked up that I feel no guilt whatsoever when harming the offending party. One of my biggest triggers is that I hate bullies. You," she paused, poking her finger forcefully against his chest, "are a bully. I can count at least five ways I can kill you right here, with just the objects available to me in this bathroom. And," she paused dramatically, leaning closer, "I will make it look like an embarrassing accident."

Stuart smiled casually and, strangely enough, no longer smelled of pepper but maybe a hint of lavender.

"Woah. You are a wild one. I like you. You're feisty," he said, taking a step closer to her so the two were so close she could now smell the tequila on his breath.

The bathroom door opened, and a tipsy man stumbled in. After letting out a loud burp, he looked up and saw Natalia and Stuart unflinchingly staring at each other, and he quickly backed out, leaving them to their private confrontation.

Stuart took a step back and held his hands in surrender. "Look, I don't want to die right now. I have too much work to do. I will head outside and apologize to your brother if that will make you feel better."

She broke eye contact and turned toward the door. "He better not find out about our little talk," she said as she left the bathroom, releasing the heavy door to close in Stuart's face.

Natalia crossed the hall and went into the woman's bathroom. She realized how much she did have to go, but, of course, there was a long line. Typical.

After finally getting her turn in a stall, she touched up her makeup, reapplied lipstick, and took a few deep breaths to calm herself before heading back out to find Daniel.

peeper the cab driver

When Natalia finally exited the lady's room, she scanned the club for Daniel. She found him standing by the end of the bar closest to the exit.

They spoke simultaneously when Natalia returned to him after weaving through the pulsing crowds.

"Can we go now?" Daniel asked.

"Are you ready to go?" Natalia said and laughed.

He nodded, held out his elbow, which she grabbed, and they walked through the dark hallway, past the bouncers, and along the long line of people waiting to get in.

Daniel hailed a taxi, and they both plopped down, dejected, in the back seat.

Most of the ride was silent. Daniel leaned his head against the window, and Natalia watched the rearview mirror as the driver attempted to look up her skirt. It was times like these she wished she had a grenade that she could carry in her purse and leave with assholes around the city.

"I'm sorry that things didn't work out how you hoped," Natalia said, looking at Daniel sympathetically. He reeked of red wine that had turned. She turned her nose up, trying to detect the smell, wondering if he had been spilled on or if that was the smell of dejection, disappointment, or maybe even depression. It was a sad smell. It made her crave a glass of wine while overwhelming her with sadness that the wine was bad. Wanting a glass of wine and not being able to drink it did sound like the perfect essence of depression.

"And yet again, all of my eggs in one basket," Daniel said, not even bothering to lift his head from the window. "Stuart did come over and offer me a drink as an apology. But it was probably spiked with something to make me act crazy, giving him and his buddies more to laugh at."

"People like that usually get what's coming to them," Natalia reassured him, thinking that she had let Stuart off the hook too easily.

Daniel's head popped up, and he angrily looked at Natalia. "What the hell does that mean? Do you think karma is going to get me a job and completely undo that embarrassing and demoralizing shit show back there? Or is it that you're going to get them?" he laughed. "Watch out, guys, or I'll sic my half-sister on you."

Natalia calmly turned her head back to the peeping cab driver and didn't reply.

Daniel sighed. "I'm sorry. I guess I am just upset. But, look, I forgot to ask. Do you have a place to stay? My apartment isn't big, but you can take the couch. It's super cozy."

Natalia smiled and moved closer to Daniel, resting her head on his shoulder. "Thanks, Daniel. That would be nice." After a few seconds of listening to the rain tap dancing on the roof, Natalia added, "Tomorrow will be a better day, I promise."

THE PROPOSITION

Natalia tiptoed out of the apartment, careful not to wake Daniel. He had such a rough night or, well, an entire day. The least she could do was grab breakfast and coffee to bring back to his place. It was a beautiful, crisp Saturday morning, and she was one of the city's first people out and about. With the sun coming up behind the tall buildings the city shone brightly, flawlessly. Each person she passed smelled of fresh cut grass. The sunrise on a new day must inspire the morning go-getters to take advantage of their fresh start.

She knew she was being followed. She could feel it. Just like she could feel people looking at her, the pressure bore down on the back of her neck. He wasn't close enough for her to hear his footsteps, but the increasing pressure of his presence told her that he would be soon. The overwhelming smell of both pepper and lavender was an unusual combination. She turned down an alley just before reaching the coffee shop. If she were an ordinary woman being followed, she would be better off heading into the coffee shop and surrounding herself with others, but average was one thing she was not. She ducked behind a surprisingly clean dumpster while listening for the approaching footsteps. Next to her foot, just under the trash bin, was a broken wine bottle. She grabbed it in her hand and held it by the neck. The footsteps grew louder and louder until a man walked right by her hiding spot. She jumped out and caught him by surprise. His high-pitched scream made it clear that he was not expecting her to jump out at him with a broken bottle.

"Holy shit. You could've given me a heart attack. What the hell are you doing back there, diddling?"

Before he even started talking, she recognized the man as the arrogant bully from the night club, Stuart "*You Do You*" Vladigan. She continued to stare at him, assessing how nervous he was.

"What are you d—" he started again, but she promptly interrupted.

"Why are you following me?"

"I saw you walking and wanted to talk to you."

She continued to stare at him until he was uncomfortable enough to speak again. She was always amazed at how the power of silence could draw information out of people.

"Okay. I looked up your brother's address from the information he gave me on his business card and followed you. But I do want to talk to you. I have a proposal for you."

"I'm listening," she said, no longer perceiving him as a threat. She tossed the wine bottle over her shoulder, making a perfect shot into the center of the dumpster.

"I couldn't sleep last night. I'm certain there was a reason why we were brought together."

"There was. You running your mouth combined with my desire to make you pay for how you treated my big brother."

"Yeah. I know. I'm sorry about that. Look, I was drinking a lot and was being an ass. I admit it, and I'm sorry. I can't stop thinking about our little interaction in the bathroom. I think you are exactly what I need for a little, uh, let's say," he searched for the right word, "project I am working on. I surmised from our conversation last night that you have particular skills and the right kind of personality I need. Honestly, I think you are perfect for what I need help with." He paused to gauge her reaction.

She stared at him, not confused, just waiting for more. No one had ever thought of her as perfect for anything. Silence ate up the seconds that passed until Stuart continued.

"I have some people I need you to take care of," he said in a whisper, winking as he spoke.

"I don't think I am the right person for that. I'm not the best caretaker. I would say you can ask my mom, but she's dead. Well, I guess that does prove my point, anyway." She looked down at her nails and started picking the dirt underneath.

"I'm not making myself clear. There are some people I need to take care of, so to speak. You know, whack them off."

"I'm not sure that means what you think that means," she responded with a sly smile.

He was uncomfortable with the conversation, and Natalia enjoyed watching him squirm.

"Tell me about them."

"What? Tell you about who?"

"The people you want me to kill. What about them?" she said without hesitation or discomfort.

Natalia held no remorse when she wronged a deserving person. Sometimes she killed animals for research, but when it came to humans, she liked to think of herself as karma's little assassin. She wouldn't lose a night of sleep after killing someone for an intolerable character flaw or aggravating habit. She was doing the world a favor. For example, sneezing once without covering your mouth could be an accident or oversight. Doing it twice is unacceptable.

The topic of murder for hire made the important man squirm. "Okay. Yikes, right to the point. These are all retired employees from my company that are pulling from our pension plan, and I noticed that—"

"No. I don't care why. I want to know about them. So, they're old? Is that it? I need some reason. They need to deserve it. A girl has to draw the line somewhere, right?"

"They're all over the country, but a large amount in the tri-state area or retired in Florida. They are all old and bleeding my company dry by pulling from the pension program. If you are a stickler for finding a reason, I am sure plenty of old people's habits will bother you enough to rationalize. Not to mention, they will probably die soon anyway," he explained. "Money is not an object. Name your price."

Natalia thought for a moment. Old people did gross her out, the smell, the blueish hair, the early dinners, and the two speeds they seemed to have: speed walking or unbearably slow. However, she was trying to be different. She was trying to change for Daniel. Indeed, this is different from the kind of thing he would approve of. Not only did she not want him to find out something she had done in her past, but she didn't want him even to know she was capable of such things. She wanted him to accept her, even if that meant changing who she was.

"Look. We can start slow. The guy in charge of our money is leaving the company. I am hoping to hire someone of my own to replace him. I need to get this rolling so that the change I am hoping to make, with your help, can appear like a happy upside to new management."

Natalia's mind was running a million miles a minute. She had so many questions. First, could she do what this man was proposing? Would this affect her relationship with Daniel? Could she use this situation to help Daniel somehow? The answers were... of course, she had been training her whole life to get rid of unnecessary people that take up space, only if he found out, and hell, yes... because she had an idea.

"I'll do what you need," she said in a level tone.

She could see the look of excitement on Stuart's face, like his plan was coming together in an unexpected but even better way than he had imagined, but he was holding back, likely sensing there was more.

"But..." she began and watched the look on his face change as he anticipated what was next. "You hire my brother for that job. If I am not mistaken, the job that he applied for and was so rudely dismissed from, might I add, is the one you need to fill."

Stuart laughed out loud, tilting his head back to the sky. "You *cannot* be serious."

With a completely straight face, she continued, "He wouldn't have approached you if he didn't think he was qualified. He's young and doesn't have experience in a company this size, but he is moldable, matches *your* brand, and most importantly, that is to be part of my compensation. You will take a chance on this young guy, watch him succeed under you, and you can both take the credit."

He saw how serious she was and paused before saying anything else.

She expected him to walk away, laugh at her again, and talk down to her like she didn't understand his business. But, instead, he smiled, and she smelled lavender. She had smelled lavender on him when she confronted him in the bathroom at the club as well. The strange thing was that it completely overpowered his previous smell of pepper, and lavender was the smell that generally came to her with admiration. It was rare that someone looked up to or respected her, but it was not a smell she would soon forget.

"Deal," he said. He stared deep into her eyes as if trying to read her soul. "I will call him in for an interview, and if I can make it work without getting fired, I will be in touch so we can get started on your tasks."

She nodded, smiled, and held out her hand. As Stuart reached out to shake, she pulled it back and added, "He can't know anything about our arrangement. Understand?"

Rather than adding the expected "You do you", he simply nodded and Natalia extended her hand. He reached out to shake it but was surprised when he found she was grabbing for the phone he was holding in his other hand. She held the phone up to his face to gain access, added her number, tossed the phone back to him, and started walking down the alley toward the main street.

"Pleasure doing business with you," he called out behind her.

Natalia rolled her eyes, wondering what she was getting into with this man... thinking about his stupid motto. You Do You. How ridiculous. Her mother had always told her never to be herself. She recalled a Saturday morning when she was a kid when she sat on the couch with her mom watching television. A Public Service Announcement came on about bullying. The message was the same as Stuart's, *Be Yourself*. Tatiana growled and threw the remote at the TV set.

"Never be yourself, Natalia. Be normal. Do you hear me?"

Natalia stared at her mother, unsure of who she was supposed to be, if not herself. "If people wanted others as they are, there wouldn't be so many people with fake information on their dating profiles. There wouldn't be so many popular filters that change your appearance when you take your picture."

"Can I be you?" Natalia asked innocently.

Tatiana laughed. "Well, you can try. It would point you in the right direction. But, even I am not myself. Don't be you. Don't be me. Be better. Be normal."

***

Stuart couldn't suppress his smile. He had recently completed writing his new code. It was a masterpiece and would help him make MBI profitable again. His *FeedingPigeons* program pulled data from human resource personnel files and other information gathered through the lax data security of the company's health care provider. The code analyzed the records, pulling out living retirees and weighing their age, medical history, pension payout, and marital status. With MBI's world-renowned generosity, not only did retirement benefit the employees, but it was passed to their spouses upon death. The program would use the breached data to generate a list of pension benefactors that, if eliminated, would reap the most financial gain. Not only had Stuart created this powerful technology to judge retired pension recipients, but his serendipitous meeting with Natalia gave him the executioner as well.

The first name generated by FeedingPigeons was Hal Smith. Hal is a sixty-three-year-old man who retired at fifty-five. The money grubber had been pulling pension payments for over eight years. The research revealed that his wife Linda's death had driven him to an early retirement. Stuart had combed through the medical reports. The prescription medication to battle depression started for Hal as soon as his wife died. Losing his life partner had put Hal into a deep depression. The increased Prozac dosage in his medical history proved how fragile Hal's psyche was. Already a diabetic, the constant heavy drinking led to alcohol-related liver disease. There were several doctor notes directing Hal to stop drinking for his health, but more recent notes in Hal's files noting his occasional confusion, drowsiness, and the yellowing of his eyes indicated he had not stopped, and cirrhosis was likely already setting in. At first glance, Stuart thought the system needed tweaking.

A person with such health concerns would likely dig their own grave. Although a chronic alcoholic, Hal was only sixty-three. *FeedingPigeons* estimated his life expectancy at closer to seventy-five. Stuart could not afford to wait another twelve years. In addition, Hal was an overachiever. That was what made him a great executive. The bastard would probably live into his nineties, and with his annual pension payout being more per year than over half of the salaried employees make, *FeedingPigeons* made a good choice.

This would be an easy mark if Natalia was as skilled as Stuart thought. He had no spouse to miss him, and with Hal's failing health, his untimely death wouldn't surprise anyone.

Stuart's best work to date, *FeedingPigeons*, would never see the light of day. The board of directors would never recognize his genius, and his doting public wouldn't be able to praise him for it. Wanting recognition was one of the reasons he started working for mainstream companies rather than hackers. With Natalia falling into his lap like a gift from God and the unanticipated benefit of hiring her brother as a clueless patsy, nothing would stop Stuart from bringing MBI back from the brink of death.

A TUrn OF LUCK

Daniel awoke to his phone vibrating across his nightstand. The sun was bright, and he could hear the hustle and bustle of the city outside his window. He glanced at the clock to see he had slept until 9:00 a.m. This was atypical for him as he was usually an early riser. However, it was also atypical for him to stay out late drinking at a club. He liked to wake up early, run, shower, dress, and still have time to stop at the coffee shop on the way to work. But now there was no work. No work and no money meant no motivation. Motivation aside, he couldn't remember the last time he slept past seven in the morning. He wondered how long he would've kept sleeping had the phone not buzzed.

He leaned over the edge of his bed, reaching to get a hold of his phone while, at the same time, trying not to fall on the floor. He answered the phone on the fourth ring, surprised the call didn't already roll into voice-mail.

"Daniel Webber speaking," he answered in a quiet voice, hoping not to wake Natalia in the other room in addition to making sure his froggy, hungover, and not-recently used voice wasn't obvious.

"Good morning, Mr. Webber," said the deep, monotone voice of what sounded like an octogenarian woman who had been smoking since she was fifteen years old. "This is Agnes Friendly, executive assistant for Stuart Vladigan at MBI."

If he wasn't wholly awake before, Daniel was wide awake now. He jolted up in bed and fought off his dizziness while he smoothed out the wrinkled t-shirt he had slept in as if Agnes could see him through the phone.

"Good morning, Ms. Friendly. What a *friendly* voice to hear first thing in the morning," he said, immediately regretting it. *Who says that?* Probably everyone makes comments like that to her, not to mention that her voice was anything *but* friendly. She probably thinks that he is mocking her. Could it be any more obvious that he was at home, in bed, sitting on his ass? By 9:00 a.m. on a typical day, he would've already been up for hours.

Agnes Friendly sighed audibly, then continued in her not-the-slightest-bit-entertained voice, "Mr. Vladigan would like you to join him for lunch tomorrow afternoon at The Green Table at 1:30 p.m. to discuss the resume he recently received from you."

Daniel was taken back to last night at the club and how Mr. Vladigan had told everyone he threw out the resume. Was it possible that it was all a test? Maybe he just wanted to see how Daniel could control himself and if he could handle himself amongst criticism.

"Thank you, Ms. Friendly. I know the place and will be there with bells on," he said, slapping himself on the forehead after hearing the call disconnect.

"With bells on? I don't know what it means, let alone why I would ever say such a thing," he muttered.

Newly invigorated, Daniel jumped up to tell Natalia in the other room, then paused as his hand grabbed the doorknob. No, he decided. He would shower, dress and make himself presentable for the big announcement. He would let her sleep until then.

LUCKY CHARM

Natalia quietly opened the door to Daniel's apartment and slowly closed it behind her, trying not to make a noise in case Daniel was still asleep.

"Did the internet teach you how to escape a hangover, too?" Daniel asked with a smile.

She jumped but recovered just in time to keep from dropping the to-go coffee cups and a bag of Danishes onto the floor. Daniel was sitting on his favorite, worn leather chair, ready to take on the world. He was a complete 180 transformation from the Daniel who moped home last night with all his dreams crushed. He was showered, shaven, dressed in crisp khakis and a pressed button-down shirt, with his hair perfectly styled. His legs were crossed, and his posture was relaxed yet confident, with both arms on the back of the wide chair.

"I wanted to let you sleep in," Natalia said, still looking shocked that he was not only up but was all put together. "I went out and got breakfast."

She handed Daniel his coffee, walked into the kitchen, and pulled out a plate to decorate with the assorted Danishes.

"Wow. You are a great roommate. Who needs a wife when you have a half-sister? Do you want to move in?"

Natalia tried to ignore the strange insinuation she was sure he didn't mean and taper down her excitement. Moving in with him, getting close to him, was precisely what she wanted. Still, it was a very odd thing to say.

"That came out weird. I meant to say thanks for breakfast. It looks amazing, and boy, did I need this coffee." He took a sip that somehow made him look even more awake. "But, why don't you plan on staying here for a while."

"But I thought you were worried you would have to move out?"

"Well," Daniel stood and walked toward the kitchen counter where Natalia sat. "I have some exciting news."

"Okay, spill. Don't make me wait."

"I have a lunch interview with Mr. Stuart Vladigan of MBI tomorrow. Can you believe it? After last night?"

"No. I can't." And she literally couldn't believe Stuart had acted so quickly. "What happened?" she asked, feigning ignorance.

"It must have all been some test. Last night at the bar... a test of character or something. He wants to talk to me about the CFO job I approached him about. What luck that I bumped into him in the bathroom after the conference. What luck that we went out. What luck that I didn't lose my temper."

What luck she didn't kill him in the bar last night. What luck she didn't slice his throat with the broken wine bottle in the alley this morning.

"I'm so happy for you! It sounds like everything is working out," she said.

"Yes. I agree. But I have you to thank, Natalia. You must be my lucky charm."

Danny Boy

Daniel tried his best not to pace in front of the hostess stand. To minimize his chances of being late, he arrived at the restaurant forty-five minutes early. He skipped coffee earlier in the morning to avoid escalating his nervous jitters. He started to walk to the men's room to splash some water on his face, but after getting halfway to the bathrooms, he changed his mind, not wanting to leave Stuart waiting should he arrive in Daniel's absence.

On his way back to the front of the restaurant, Daniel caught a glimpse of Stuart walking through the large double doors, waving enthusiastically. His casual demeanor gave Daniel the optimistic feeling that this interview would be excellent. *A test.* He had to keep reminding himself that every-thing that happened at the club was just a test. *There is no need to be nervous.* Stuart was waving at him and looked happy to see him. *There is nothing to be worried about.* Daniel waved back with an animated smile and picked up his pace.

Before he arrived at the hostess stand, Daniel watched and cringed as Stuart grabbed the hostess in a friendly embrace. Realizing Stuart's over-excited wave was intended for her, not him, caused Daniel's forehead and upper lip to break out in sweat beads. As he took his last few steps toward the man who could decide his future, Daniel dabbed at his face with his sleeve and tried to push the embarrassment down, hoping not to appear completely red-faced and sweaty.

"Daniel-san!" Stuart exclaimed. "I wondered for a moment if you may be running late."

"Oh, no," the hostess said with a wink. "He has been here at least thirty minutes."

Daniel didn't know if he should be thankful to her for covering for his absence or angry because it was clear that she was making fun of him. Before he could respond, Stuart clapped him on the back, practically knocking the wind out of him, and said, "This way. I have a special table with a standing reservation."

Stuart seemed to know someone at every table they walked past.

"Can you believe that ballgame?" said one guy.

"Heard you killed it at the conference," another said.

"Hey, Sexy man," came from a rather old but frisky-looking woman.

It took them what felt like fifteen minutes to walk to their table; all the time, Daniel just hung in the background twiddling his thumbs with a fake, uncomfortable grin. He tried not to look too awkward and would laugh when they laughed, but it was tough to keep up since he couldn't follow half of what they were talking about.

Finally, the two men sat down and ordered their lunch. When the waiter left the table, Daniel saw his chance to impress his potential boss and steer the conversation.

"Mr. Vladigan, I saw the feature piece in the New World Business Journal. It's simply amazing how you have impacted MBI's bottom line in such a short time. The naysayers thought it would be like turning a ship, but you have made progress quickly."

Stuart grinned modestly and whispered, "That was only half the story." He paused, took a sip of his water, and smacked his lips. "They left out that I straight up fired a large number of employees for cause so I wouldn't have to pay them a severance. It doesn't take much to prove cause... departments are not meeting their goals... literally missing their financial targets by 50 percent or more... plus no one wants to battle our legal team."

Daniel interjected without thinking. "Wasn't that bad for morale?"

If he was trying to make a good impression, he needed to watch everything he said. The last thing he needed was for his comments to put Stuart on the defensive.

"As soon as morale starts bringing in revenue, let me know. Until then, please don't question my business moves. Leaders can't be afraid of difficult conversations or tough decisions. Morale is not a tangible measurement. Profit and revenue are."

Stuart again reached for his water, drinking it all down like a shot of liquor. "The article also mentioned the ending of the pension program, but they conveniently left out the fact that we bought out as many pensions as we could. But, thousands of retirees remain to suck our would-be profits from us without contributing."

Stuart paused briefly as the waiter filled their water glasses and walked away. "Daniel, one of the brilliant things about numbers and math is that they're black and white. But, in finance, there are some gray areas. If I hire you, and I just might, you could learn from me and how I deal with those gray areas. I can teach you to control what you can and influence what you can't control."

As if he turned a switch, Stuart abruptly changed the topic and began speaking about everything under the sun other than the job. Whenever

Daniel would bring up MBI or the job hoping to show off his knowledge of the industry, Stuart would immediately change the topic to something bizarre, asking questions like, "Do you think the moon landing was a hoax?" or "Have you ever tried ketchup on your eggs?"

Two waiters arrived with drink refills and the ordered meals. Daniel was relieved to have a natural break to hopefully get an opportunity to reset the conversation or even to have an excuse for silence while he chewed.

The waiter placed Stuart's giant surf and turf plate on the table in front of him. The filet was as tall as it was fat, and the lobster was so massive it hung slightly off the plate. Stuart bent forward, placed his nose almost entirely against the steak, and took a long-satisfied sniff, rolling his eyes back in his head. He growled and winked at Daniel, which for some reason, reminded him of the first time he met Natalia in the coffee shop and the audible love affair she had with her cinnamon bun and hot chocolate.

The second waiter placed Daniel's roasted apple and brie sandwich in front of him, saying, "Enjoy your lunch."

Daniel replied, "You too." *Ugh, why do I always do that?* Daniel thought to himself, looking up to see if Stuart noticed. Stuart, fortunately, was too captivated by his meal to notice anything else. While Daniel was embarrassing himself with the waiter, Stuart had tied on a bib and was now staring at his food with his fingers dancing in the air as he looked back and forth, unsure what to tackle first.

After five minutes of eating in silence, Stuart placed his napkin across his half-eaten meal, took a sip of his drink, and said, "I want to hire you, Daniel."

Daniel, so taken by surprise, gasped and, when doing so, inhaled a small crumb from the crusty bread of his sandwich. He tried to hold back his cough, but the tickle in his throat was not to be ignored. Daniel coughed politely but still, rather violently, into his sleeve. He reached for his glass of water only to be once again overtaken by the overwhelming urge to cough. His eyes began to water, and his face got hot. When he was finally able to take a sip of water, he realized he was close to dripping with sweat. A bead ran down his temple, he felt the liquid accumulating on his lip, and he also felt a drop run down the small of his back, right into his butt crack. He glanced up at Stuart, unsure what reaction his coughing fit would have conjured, but Stuart was casually leaning back in his chair, staring at him with a coy smile.

"Look. I want to hire you as my new CFO. Old man Johnson will finally retire this Friday. I need you to show up to work Monday morning ready to go. We are going to make big changes together, Danny Boy."

Stuart stood, clapped Daniel on the back, nearly triggering another coughing fit, and continued, "The bill is paid for, and I have somewhere I need to be. How weird is this? I am meeting with an old retired MBI dude about piloting my private jet. True story, his name is Dick Hertz. I shit you not. Dick Hertz still suckling from the pension teet."

Resuming his relaxed position, Stuart paused as if pondering the universe before continuing, "It's a small world."

"Or a big company," Daniel quipped, gaining confidence.

Stuart laughed, then continued, "I'm not sure why I waste my time meeting with him. It sounds like with the technology these days, the airplanes practically fly themselves."

Daniel stood awkwardly with his napkin falling to the floor from his lap and reached out his hand, saying, "Thank you, Mr. Vladigan. I will not let you down." Only to be met with Stuart's fist bump.

Stuart looked down, clearly amused, at his fist being shaken by Daniel's hand and laughed, "Please, call me Stuart." He turned, walked toward the exit, and then called over his shoulder, "See you Monday. Be there at 7:00 a.m."

***

Stuart had no interest in hiring Daniel. He despised young professionals like him. Yes, Daniel had an Ivy League degree but needed more creativity. His resume was littered with the buzzwords that Stuart hated. The CV boasted his accomplishments with terms like *synergy, ownership, proactive, accountability,* and a dozen others. What the resume didn't have was originality. Daniel was everything Stuart was *not* looking for in a CFO. But Stuart was willing to make Daniel his pawn to get what he needed. Natalia was the queen of the game and would be the one to help him make a difference in MBI's financial future.

With the intensity of working in such a high-profile position, Daniel would doubtlessly fizzle out within a year. Stuart wasn't afraid to play the long game. It was part of his brilliance.

STREET GYROS

I t was a crisp fall morning, and as Natalia exited the subway stairs from the dank and dirty underground, she noticed how this part of town was so clean and shiny. Not only did the buildings reach higher into the sky but the sidewalks were less pocked from wear and discarded gum than the other side of town. Everything was more businesslike than residential and even the sprinkling of bars and restaurants were cleaner and classy.

As she walked a block further, Natalia appreciated how the street vendors differed. Rather than the hot dog and tamale vendors that frequent other neighborhoods, the variety of selections was astounding. There was a pretzel vendor, a Gyro cart, and even a quaint wagon selling gourmet pastries. She was tempted to stop and sample some selections from the posh side of town but then remembered that her entire purpose of the trip was to eat with Daniel.

Natalia planned to meet him at the restaurant he suggested, but he was so excited about his new job, office, and shiny skyscraper that he begged her to meet him at his office. She thought it was cute that he wanted to show off for her.

Upon entering the mirrored skyscraper, she stopped and looked up. The lobby ceiling had to be at least four stories tall. She wondered who changed those light bulbs and how they managed. The shiny exterior of the building was equally matched, if not surpassed, by the elegant interior.

And it wasn't just the marble walls and floors that gave off a luxurious ambiance or the metal escalators and elevator doors that were somehow void of any fingerprints whatsoever, even the people looked pressed and polished. The security staff wore intimidating military-like uniforms but expressed a helpful and welcoming vibe. The men and women passing through the lobby wore high-fashion suits she could only imagine were custom tailored. She had to fight the urge to touch the fabric or lean in for a sniff. These people probably smelled fantastic. She longed to recognize the smell of the upper echelon.

While the friendly and handsome security guard called up to alert Daniel of her arrival, she concluded that the security guards must be out-of-work actors or models. Natalia was directed to the central bank of elevators and the top floor. When she stepped on the elevator with a small group of others, they all stared at her curiously as she pressed the button for her floor. The elevator rode straight to the seventieth floor before making its first stop. She glanced back at the controls and noticed that the elevator she was on only stopped at floors seventy through eighty. It must be rare for people to ride to the top floor the way her fellow riders continued to stare. She began to feel self-conscious, considering she was wearing jeans with a graphic tee and hardly fit the description of an executive or even an assistant. She may have been able to pass as a delivery person, except for her empty hands.

The last person exited the elevator on the seventy-fifth floor after giving her an envious smile.

Natalia leaned after him hoping to smell his success, but she only smelled vodka.

When the elevator doors opened, Natalia was greeted by a tall, thin, and beautiful woman who called her by name.

"Welcome, Natalia. Please take a seat. Mr. Webber is on his way up from his office. May I offer you a drink while you wait?" She gestured to the showroom-type lounge area to the right.

"No, thank you," Natalia replied, sitting in a high-back leather chair. Less than a minute later, the elevator doors opened, and Daniel emerged.

"There's my girl!" Daniel said rather loudly, walking toward Natalia with open arms.

After the awkward embrace, she looked at him and said, "Wait. Why did I come to this floor if your office is not here?"

"Very observant, Natalia." He laughed. "I am an executive, which means my office should be on this floor. But I opted to have my office down in the trenches with the everyday man. However, my executive assistant is up here with the rest of the executive team, so my meetings are normally up in the executive conference room; my guests are directed to this floor, and I often use the executive lounge and bathrooms up here. They're way nicer."

She had her answer if Natalia wondered how often a person could use the word executive in a sentence.

"Let's head down to my floor, and I'll show you my office before we go," Daniel said, pointing back to the elevator.

The sparkly doors opened, and Stuart Vladigan strutted off the elevator.

"Danny Boy! So nice of you to bless us with your presence on this floor." Stuart looked over toward Natalia, feigning not to recognize her. "And, who is this beautiful specimen?" Stuart reached for her hand, but rather than shaking it, turned it over and kissed the back without breaking eye contact. She had to give it to him; he was suave and confident, having no trouble hitting on someone young enough to be his daughter.

"Stuart, this is my half-sister, Natalia. She was at the club with me that night after the conference," Daniel said in a less-than-confident, shaky voice.

Stuart dropped her hand gently, with his eyes still upon hers, "How could I ever forget? I am so ashamed. I was an embarrassment that evening. Please accept my deepest apologies for my behavior."

The elevator doors started to close until Stuart held his arm out to hold them open. "It was nice to see you again, Natalia," he said with a wink as she and Daniel walked onto the waiting elevator.

Stuart had held up his end of the bargain. Natalia knew she would have to start her end soon, but today was about lunch with her big brother.

Daniel's office was on the sixty-eighth floor, which meant they had to ride the elevator back to the lobby and transfer to another bank of elevators that serviced that floor. As they rode up the new elevator non-stop to his floor, Natalia was immediately aware that although the elevator was equally fingerprint-free, this elevator somehow seemed like a downgrade from the one that traveled to the top floor. When the doors opened, it was clear that the same was true for the sixty-eighth-floor lobby. Although clean and very nice, everything from the floors and artwork to the reception area and lounge was a step down from the top floor.

Natalia trailed behind Daniel as he fist-bumped or high-fived every person he passed. Some people he called by name, but the ones he didn't know, he referred to as guy, buddy, or lady. It was painful to watch as not many people wanted to be fist-bumped or high-fived. Their body language was easy to read as they leaned away from Daniel to avoid contact.

When they entered his office, he walked behind the desk, sat in his oversized chair, leaned back with his hands behind his head, and propped his feet up on the desk. "I like to consider myself a man of the people. I don't like to think of myself as a high-level executive. I'm much younger than most of the executive team, so I like to be down here with my people."

Natalia smiled and felt happy to see him so proud, but she wondered how many people on this floor saw him that way. She took a seat in one of the plush chairs on the opposite side of the desk and took in the surroundings. Regardless of what floor this office was on, she was sure that most employees did not have the budget for such lavish furnishings. The desk and bookshelves looked like solid works of art rather than furniture bought in bulk from an office supply store. The bookshelves were less than functional. There needed to be finance or business books within reach, and none were in sight. However, there were two framed Ivy League School diplomas; a BS and an MBA, a baseball encased in a glass cube with a black signature across the front, a random plate on a stand of some sort, and of course, a framed photo of his mother.

"You look like you settled in quickly. Your office is already decorated, and you seem to know lots of people."

Daniel removed his feet from his desk and leaned forward toward Natalia. "It's tough to remember all the names. All of those people have one person to meet, me. I have to meet every one of them and remember their names. I don't want to be one of those high-level guys who doesn't know anyone's name." He lowered his voice. "A little secret between you and me," he glanced over her shoulder toward the door, "If I forget someone's name, I call them something generic, like *buddy*. It's foolproof." He leaned back again and laughed.

Foolproof if no one notices, Natalia thought to herself. However, she recognized his tactic in the first minute and was sure she couldn't be the only one.

"So, how long do you have for lunch?"

Daniel laughed out loud. "I can come and go as I please. I am the freaking CFO. I can take the whole afternoon off if I want."

"Great! Let's have lunch, then do something fun." Natalia called his bluff, surprised at the change in his attitude from just a week ago when he had no job.

"I would, but I have so many things to get on top of, having just started. Lots to do. I am sure you understand."

"Of course. Where should we have lunch then? I saw some fancy street vendors."

"Street vendors? Natalia, I am taking you someplace nice. I wanted to take you to Posh. It is amazing. You have to be *somebody* to get in. Stuart introduced me yesterday so that I can get in now."

"Wow, that sounds nice—" Natalia started before Daniel cut her off.

"Unfortunately, I accidentally knocked down a waiter holding two full trays of food and drinks, so I think I need to let some time pass before I head back. I hate to disappoint you, but maybe I can take you there next time."

Natalia shrugged, thinking she would be okay with a street gyro.

JUST a PreTTy Face?

Natalia walked silently through the large and mostly empty room toward a frail woman standing at the windows overlooking the city below. Light instrumental music played peacefully throughout the room; the candles lit throughout smelled of cinnamon. She slowly pulled the choke wire out of her pocket and quietly pulled it to its full length, spanning from her left hand to her right, shoulder-width apart. With only one more step between herself and her soon-to-be victim, she raised the wire to loop it over the large, bluish-grey, perfectly coiffed hairdo. As the choke wire fell around the woman's neck and Natalia pulled the wire taught, she caught the reflection in the window and found herself staring at her bitch of a mother. Suddenly, she was not choking her mom or anyone, but she was holding on to the reigns of a bucking bronco in a sleazy bar surrounded by zoo animals singing Christmas carols. A rhino in a tight mini-skirt and a bedazzled bustier cheered her on while a penguin honked foul pickup lines in her direction.

She awoke drenched in sweat, her muscles aching from the challenging bull ride. Her dreams tended to go from realistic and often on a deep subconscious level to extremely odd and entertaining.

***

Two weeks later, the inevitable meeting to kick off her part of the arrangement had arrived. Natalia found herself in an elevator riding up to the penthouse floor of an exclusive residential building. She found it odd that the black and white nude photos hung on the walls seemed like a highly personal touch for a building elevator before realizing that this elevator was actually private.

When the doors opened, she was greeted by a woman who resembled the subject of the erotic elevator art. Natalia recognized her as the woman from the club who had been sitting with Stuart looking on disapprovingly while he was making an ass of himself.

"Natalia," the woman said in a kind voice, gently grabbing Natalia's hands with both of hers. "My name is Bunny. It's nice to finally meet you."

Bunny's hands were smooth with beautifully manicured nails and at least a dozen bangle bracelets clanging around her wrist, yet her handshake was firm and professional. Her warm smile instantly put Natalia at ease, though she was still unsure how much this woman knew about her "new role."

Bunny turned to direct Natalia to their large sitting room overlooking the vast city below and asked, "What can I get you to drink? A cocktail? Sparkling water? Wine?"

Natalia had just finished a pumpernickel bagel with strawberry cream cheese and a large coffee before coming over. She, therefore, passed on the drink and the delectable display of muffins on the coffee table next to the enormous sectional sofa where they finally sat.

While Bunny answered a quick text on her phone, Natalia took in her surroundings. The place was like nowhere she had ever been. She couldn't believe people lived like this. What stood out the most was the enormous

You Do You neon sign on the wall. She shook her head in disbelief. It was a hint of tackiness in an otherwise elegantly decorated room.

Natalia chuckled, then looked back at Bunny. "Is Stuart coming?"

"I'm sorry, but no. He had to head out of town on business this morning. Even though you will be working for him, your official title will be my assistant to explain any meetings and conversations with me. I'll meet with you when necessary. Information will flow from his software program, to him, to me and finally to you"

Natalia was pleasantly surprised at Bunny's professionalism and organization, but she couldn't help but wonder how much the woman knew about Natalia's agreement with Stuart. She watched as Bunny pulled out a large shopping bag and placed it on the table.

"In this bag, you will find a variety of tools..." she said, using finger quotes, "...which you can use with your assignments. First, you will find a new cell phone to use as my assistant."

Natalia pulled out the phone and turned it on.

"You may use this for any business dealings with Stuart or me. Preloaded in your contact book are all my contacts so you can make reservations for me, schedule appointments, order a limo, book the private jet, and so forth." Bunny paused, watching Natalia to see if she was following her direction and waiting to see if she would object.

Natalia knew there would be more, so she made a mental note to save her objections for Stuart.

"I'll share the contacts to the phone of the clientele you need to *meet.*" Bunny did not use air quotes, but her facial expression fell slightly as she emphasized the last word. "The first contact has already been added, Harold Smith."

Natalia opened the contacts app and scrolled to the listing for Harold Smith. Along with his name were an address, phone number, email address, photo, and notes. The notes detailed personal information, such as his favorite restaurant, where he dines alone almost nightly, and the country club where he plays golf three to four days a week. She glanced up at Bunny, waiting for more.

"You'll use this information to take care of your business. I would still suggest deleting the contact when you have completed your assignment. Text me when you are ready for the next contact; my number is also listed on your phone."

Bunny stopped again, checking to be sure she didn't lose Natalia somewhere in the conversation. Natalia stayed silent without breaking eye contact.

"Okay, I also have a notebook that contains all the information you need about me, from my favorite brands, online accounts, shoe size, allergies, and more. It would help if you kept this on you at all times. The notebook is in a new custom leather bag I had made for you as a token of my thanks, along with a bottle of champagne."

She smiled, and Natalia smiled back for the first time since she sat. This woman was on top of things. She was smart, kind, efficient, and hard not to like. *But did Bunny know all the details of her arrangement?* Natalia wondered again. At the very least, the bombshell beauty played the "plausible deniability" card, and she did so with style and class.

Bunny stood, and Natalia took it as her cue to leave. They walked back to the elevator, where Bunny eagerly hugged her. It was only slightly awkward since Bunny was at least a foot taller than Natalia in her heels, so Bunny's rock-solid boobs hit Natalia right in the throat.

karma is a bitch

Natalia grabbed a coffee on her way home and sat in the park. She didn't need or even want another cup, but sitting in the park without something to do was suspicious. She loved watching the people going about their day, not knowing how easily they could die. She would imagine all of the "accidents" that could happen to each person, yet they would walk by completely unaware.

She sipped her coffee and thought back to her meeting earlier with Bunny. Natalia was surprised that she liked her. At first glance, one would assume Bunny was a spoiled, ditzy blonde with fake boobs who could get anything she wanted by batting her long lashes and jiggling her supple tits. But after sitting with her for less than a half hour, Natalia realized that, yes, Bunny is beautiful and her tits are most definitely fake, but that she is an intelligent businesswoman who is also generous and kind.

***

She thought back to the popular, pretty girls in high school. They were indeed not generous or kind. Sure, they would talk to her and throw out fake compliments right before homecoming court voting, but a week later, they would forget she existed. Natalia was unsure if they ignored her out of fear or were indifferent.

The same girls she would hear laughing at her for wearing sunglasses during PE class and sometimes even inside the school due to her light sensitivity would complement her glasses when they needed something... like an extra quarter for ice cream on Fridays or to switch seats so they could sit next to their crush.

When one of the pretty girls, like Allison, would start a simple conversation in class, Natalia would screw it up with her weirdness.

"Hey, Natalia, do you have an extra pencil? Mine broke, and the sharpener isn't working. Debbie was going to grab one from her locker, but she isn't back yet."

"Sure," Natalia would say, not sure she was entirely hiding her excitement of being spoken to. "You can use mine, but don't worry about Debbie. I can smell her just outside in the hall."

Allison turned toward the door, and sure enough, Debbie walked through. Debbie had the smell of salt water, pity. It wasn't unpleasant, but it reminded Natalia of her tears. Debbie always got whatever she wanted, but she was still human enough to realize that most people did not. Maybe that is why she seemed to pity everyone else.

Natalia held her pencil out to Allison, but Allison flinched and pulled her arm back like Natalia was holding a venomous snake.

"Uh, thanks. It looks like Debbie has one for me."

The actions following encounters like this were always the same—a fake laugh, a forced smile. They would angle their body away from her as if that extra inch of space kept them immune from Natalia's weirdness.

She often heard conversations die down or the subject change when she approached the groups of pretty girls. She considered herself lucky that they didn't tease her to her face anymore, but the fact that they wanted nothing to do with her was painfully clear.

***

When Natalia first laid eyes on Bunny in the club, she was sure she was just like those girls, but then she saw a glimpse of sympathy over how her husband treated Daniel. Even when she showed up at the penthouse, not expecting to meet with Bunny, she was surprised—assuming she would talk down to her, avoid her, and treat her like a freak. But she didn't. Bunny was beautiful, and she knew how to use her so-called assets. But she was also intelligent and considerate and didn't hide it.

Natalia wondered what it would be like to embrace the things that made her different rather than hide them or be in an ongoing battle with herself to change. Her big brother was all she had now, but there was no way he could ever find out what she was like deep inside, what she had done, and what she planned to do... for him. She committed to be the person he expected her to be... or at least let him see what he wanted.

She stared at two women walking by her park bench in their yoga pants and tank tops, both carrying large water bottles. What were they talking about? Did they confide their oddities to each other, or did they pretend they were someone else like people do online? She imagined for a bit what it would feel like to walk with Bunny and share stories, laugh and cry but know that she wasn't being judged. But the more she watched the women, the more obvious it was that their conversation was just a time filler between when they would glance down at their phones or smartwatch. They were not smiling and laughing with each other; they were smiling and laughing about whatever notification they just received. What kind of sick relationship did these women have with each other, both spending more time looking at their phones than each other, or even in front of them, to where they were going?

Almost as if Natalia willed it to happen, one of the women stumbled briefly while glancing at her phone, then continued walking while glancing around quickly to see if anyone noticed. Natalia smiled, imagining the situation ending differently, with the woman's skull cracked open on the sidewalk. *It would serve her right. Karma is a bitch.*

A-HOLE IN ONE

Since Daniel started his new job, Natalia had seen little of him. It was all for the better, though, because she had been spending time at the golf course. She watched her mark, Harold Smith, paid attention to how he treated the staff, spied on his foursome from the turn, and listened to how he spoke with friends after a round of golf. Harold seemed to live most of his life with a drink in his hand, no matter the time of day, which aligned with the information Stuart's program provided her through Bunny's contacts. Harold, although inebriated most of the time, was a creature of habit. He golfed every weekday morning with three of his buddies. Tee time was 9:45 a.m., with a cooler filled with enough beer for the front nine, followed by a tall glass of bourbon at the turn. It was like clockwork.

If there was one thing she learned while observing, it was that Harold was a Grade-A asshole. He spoke down to everyone on staff but especially to the women. If there were women on the course, he spoke to them like they were not supposed to be there; if they *had* to be, they should yield to him. He was also quite the grab-ass with any young waitress or bar cart driver. Natalia had no problem finding reasons to rid the world of the sexist pig. Plus, he distinctly smelled of urine.

Natalia donned a sleeveless, white polo shirt and short black skort, threw on a black visor and oversized sunglasses, and stepped into a role as a bar cart assistant. From what she learned from her trainer, Robin, driving the bar cart and serving the golfers is just a one-person job. Still, due to the on-going questionable behavior of some very wealthy clients, the club decided that there was safety—and witnesses—in numbers, and they would send a trainee with each bar cart attendee.

For the most part, Natalia sat in the passenger seat of the golf cart and smiled, only helping when Robin needed it. Most golfers were grateful to the bar cart drivers, and they were also kind and amazing tippers. But, when they arrived at the turn, where Harold and his cronies were stocking up for the back nine, Robin stopped us before whispering a warning:

"These guys drink a lot and don't think anything about brushing up against you or even throwing the random butt slap, so just be sure not to get too close. And, whatever you do, do not bend over in front of them."

Natalia was thankful to Robin for her warning, however unnecessary it was. Natalia witnessed his behavior and was aware of the kind of person she was eliminating.

"Hey guys, the beer wenches are here!" one of the men Natalia soon identified as Harold yelled.

"Ugh. Just smile and hope for big tips," Robin whispered like a ventriloquist through a clenched-teeth smile.

As they pulled to a stop, Robin directed Natalia to stay in the cart with a look all women are familiar with. Her eyes said, "I got you girl!"

"Hi, folks. How's your round going today?" Robin stepped off the cart but did not approach the group.

"Oh, you know how it is. A bad day at golf is better than a good day at work. Not that any of us work anymore," said a tall, bald, and thin man, getting a laugh from the others.

Robin grabbed three beer bottles from the cooler and brought them to the three men walking toward her.

Although it was barely eleven in the morning, a voice from the pack of men could be heard saying, "It's five o'clock somewhere!"

"Thank you, Robin. Keep the change," the tall man said, handing her a fifty-dollar bill for the drinks as Harold approached.

"What the hell are you tipping her for, Jack? She gave you a beer, not a blow job." Harold laughed loudly at his crude joke. After catching his breath from laughing, he put his arm around Robin, letting his hand dangle over her breast, and whispered something into her ear.

"Yes, sir," Robin said, turning bright red. She turned around, poured him a bourbon and Coke—very heavy on the bourbon—and handed the drink with a fully extended arm, hoping to create some distance.

"Just take mine out of that big fat tip."

Then right as Robin turned around, clearly thinking Harold was walking off, he reached back and gave her a swift smack on her backside. He turned on his heel and laughed as he walked away.

In this day and age, Natalia was unsure how anyone could get away with behaving like that without a harassment suit. She supposed the girls needed the tips and knew that when push came to shove, the club would likely take the word of a high-paying member over an hourly employee.

Natalia consoled Robin as they returned the beer cart. "You handled that whole situation with great constraint and class. Thanks for shielding me from that group, but I'm a big girl, and I can handle myself. I'll take the bullet tomorrow with them. We can alternate, share the pain and the big tips," she winked.

***

In high school, Natalia dabbled in experiments with poison. She tested various combinations on her neighbor's cats. Ms. Shelly Bonham, or as Natalia and her mom liked to call her, Mrs. Jellybottom, regularly fed at least a dozen feral cats. Natalia would tag one with a dot of black spray paint to know on which she was currently experimenting. She tried rat poison, antifreeze, weed killer, and other chemicals she found when she would sneak into Jellybottom's basement.

Natalia kept a journal buried in her backyard in a small plastic bin where she would track the results. She recognized that it didn't take much to do the job and that she had to be very careful, or the cat would die too quickly or gruesomely. Only once did she not dispose of the specimen before Jellybottom found the cat's corpse. Fortunately, the morbidly obese old lady just assumed the cat rummaged through someone's garbage and "got into somethin' nasty." She came to expect that the other cats would come and go, and Natalia didn't even think she knew which cat was which.

The fun part for her came when she started to experiment on people. She knew she had to be very careful with testing dosages. She once slipped some eye drops into a pretty girl's protein shake. Less than an hour later, Sasha was sent home. Rumor had it her diarrhea had shut down the girl's bathroom on the second floor for three days.

The downside, however, was that she was caught a week or so later. Coach Cooley, the favorite PE teacher, was out on his daily walk one evening. He happened upon Natalia in the alley holding a cat by the neck and dropping a liquid into its mouth with a syringe. He was a large man, not overweight, but a genuine athlete. Despite his size, the man moved like a ninja. Natalia hadn't even heard him coming.

"Natalia!" he shouted from only a few feet behind her. "What are you doing to that poor cat?"

Natalia knew there was no use hiding the cat behind her back. The damage had been done. She offered up no excuses. She stared into his sad, disappointed eyes while taking in the familiar smell of spoiled red wine.

Coach Cooley sighed and looked down at his feet. "Take me to your mother," he said, sounding like it was something he wanted even less than she did.

Natalia opened the back gate and walked him through the backyard toward the house. She sensed his attention wavering as they approached the back door. This strong, confident man had seen something in their yard that nearly brought him to tears.

"Well, hello," Tatiana purred seductively as she watched Coach Cooley approach.

"Good evening, ma'am. I'm sorry to visit at such a late hour, but I just witnessed your daughter torturing a poor cat in the back alley. And, after what happened last week at school..." He could hardly finish. "I don't want to tell anyone. I don't want to ruin her life because of a childish mistake. But I want you to pull her from the school or get her some serious help. Or I will," he said, turned, and jogged out of the yard.

The whole back porch smelled of tainted, rotten, sour red wine. Natalia dreaded telling the entire tale to her mom. She even wondered if she lied, would her mother believe her? But Tatiana wanted no explanation. She assumed whatever it was, was bad enough to make a stink around town. She returned to the house and wrote a letter to the school, pulling her out citing her fictional desire to homeschool. The entire episode smelled of disappointment for Natalia's mom without a hint of surprise. The homeschooling itself was made up of Natalia watching videos on her own. The setup was mutually beneficial as Tatiana didn't have to do any work, and Natalia had her mom out of her hair. That was until Tatiana got nosey and found Natalia's notebook of cat poison experiments. There was no stern talk or punishment except for the removal or paining over any mirrors in Natalia's bedroom, so she didn't even have herself as company.

So, technically, Natalia wasn't kicked out of school. But she had no choice in the matter. She had no chance to defend herself. Not that there was a reasonable defense, but it would've been nice to be asked.

***

When Natalia returned to the country club days later, she made her way into the staff locker room, then out the side door to the already prepped bar cart anticipating the upcoming rounds for Harold's crew. The bottle of bourbon that sat on the cart was only half full. Natalia added just enough antifreeze, which she brought with her in a thermos, to the bottle to ensure a large enough dose to inflict severe damage and hopefully immediate death but not to alter the taste or color of the drink.

With Harold being a lifelong diabetic, Natalia went the antifreeze route, knowing that the main effect of the poison would be kidney failure. She would have no problem slitting the man's throat or cutting off his balls, but Natalia wanted something more subtle.

Natalia watched as the regular group of guys approached the turn. She hopped in the cart and pulled away from the bar and closer to the hole, catching a thankful smile from Robin as she passed by. Natalia winked back at the girl and drove off. It wouldn't be fun and was against the club's new rules, but she felt better dealing with the skeezy men alone. Nothing was worse than watching someone accept sexual assault because they need a job.

A mere twenty minutes later, Natalia was getting into her rental car. Her next stop would be a gas station where she could dump the thermos and bourbon bottle that sat upright in the passenger seat.

Shouts echoed through the previously peaceful morning. Rather than head for the exit, Natalia pulled the car around the circular drive of the country club in hopes of catching a glimpse of her handy work.

A golf cart rounded the side of the building through the grass and hopped the curb; the driver holding tightly to the shirt of a passenger who appeared to be unconscious. Harold's limp body bounced to the right and dangled over the edge of the cart, his arm only inches away from dragging on the asphalt drive. The driver released Harold momentarily to grab the wheel with both hands and navigate around Natalia's car. Without the counterweight of the driver's grasp, Harold flopped to the ground in a heap. His body rolled over twice before it came to a stop, revealing his oversized gut.

The driver jumped from his cart and began to run over to Harold before realizing he hadn't engaged the break. He turned to chase the cart as it picked up speed, rolling down the hill directly toward the parking lot packed with luxury vehicles.

Natalia barked out a one syllable laugh. The guy would never make it in time. He was in better shape than Harold, but he was no spring chicken. She actually wanted to see him catch it and try to jump back on, but Natalia knew she needed to leave the scene.

Pulling the car slowly around Harold's body, she took one final glance. His shirt was pulled up to his neck where his face looked visibly swollen. Whether the swelling was caused by the fall or his kidney failure, she didn't care. Harold's eyes were only slightly open, being forced closed by his enlarged face. As Natalia passed by, she saw the dying man blink. She smiled at him and pulled away.

But, as she turned her car away from the club, she grimaced at the approaching bright, flashing lights of an ambulance in her rearview mirror. Her stomach dropped as she realized the emergency workers may actually get there in time to save him. Natalia punched the steering wheel. She missed the perfect opportunity to run the guy over, but with his gut rising higher than a speed bump she could've gotten the car stuck. She took a deep breath and hoped she hadn't failed her first assignment.

DEBRIEF

Stuart sat on a squeaky stool in a hole-in-the-wall dive called Club Foot, nursing a stale beer. The bar was dark and dirty; it smelled like stale urine, played shit music, and currently, he was the only patron. He reached under his seat to move his stool closer to the counter when his fingers touched something sticky. He flinched and wiped his hands on his jeans, finding it odd that he hoped it was gum. The door to the bar opened and closed with a high-pitched screech followed by the loud bang of a door due to an over-tightened closer. Stuart watched as Natalia walked over. She met his gaze but then immediately looked to her feet. He planned to meet her to celebrate, but she looked prepared to give him bad news.

"So," Natalia started before she even sat down, "what does this mean for Daniel?"

"Nice to see you, too, Natalia," Stuart said playfully. "Can I get you a drink?"

"Daniel doesn't know anything about this. He can NEVER know anything about this. You understand that, right?" Natalia said in a direct and forceful whisper while leaning closer to Stuart's face.

"What's got your panties in a bunch?" Stuart said as he took another sip from his bottle.

"You came to me, right? It was your idea. Daniel has nothing to do with this. It was my first try, and maybe I didn't dose him enough, even though he drank so much," she said, looking up at the ceiling as if pondering her actions. "And fell off a speeding golf cart," Natalia added as an afterthought.

Stuart stared at her, confused, until Natalia snapped back to the moment and continued, "I don't know how he was still alive when I left. But, the ambulance arrived quicker than I anticipated" She sat on the wobbly barstool next to Stuart and looked down at her hands on her lap.

Stuart watched her as she wrung her hands, and, every minute or so, she chewed on her fingernails. She looked even younger in her vulnerable state and Stuart wondered if the other people in the bar thought he was a shitty parent having brough his daughter with him or a dirty old man. He took a sip of beer and glanced over her shoulder at the muted television on the far wall. He reached over and casually pulled her hand away from her mouth.

"This is all new to me, but I would think that biting your nails is an occupational hazard in your line of work," Stuart said.

She lifted her eyes to meet his gaze just as he cupped her chin and gently turned her head just enough so that she could see the tv. The screen showed an aerial shot of the country club with the bottom ticker reading: GOLFER DIES OF APPARENT ALCOHOL POISONING.

With her mouth agape, Natalia whipped her head around to look at Stuart. "He's dead?" she said and looked back at the screen, now showing a journalist interviewing one of the bar cart girls. The volume was still muted due to the loud music that was playing.

She read the closed captioning, scrolling across the bottom: REPORTER: WAS HE HERE OFTEN? WHAT WAS HE LIKE?"

WOMAN: 'YES. HE WAS... REGULAR.

REPORTER: HOW DID HE SEEM WHEN YOU SAW HIM?

WOMAN: HE WAS THE WAY HE USUALLY WAS [COUGH]. I HAVE NEVER SEEN ANYONE DRINK THAT MUCH EACH AND EVERY MORNING. HE STARTED DRINKING BEER LIKE WATER BEFORE TEN.

Stuart kept his eyes on her, already aware of what she was just now realizing.

"One down."

Natalia looked back to Stuart with a smile. "I think I will have that drink. Anything but bourbon."

BUNNY'S DAY OUT

With her eyes barely open, Natalia rolled over on the couch and grasped her vibrating cell phone off the coffee table.

"Good morning, boss," she mumbled into the phone while wiping the sleep from her eyes.

"Meet me outside your place in five," Bunny ordered in a firm yet sweet-sounding voice.

"Yes, ma'am," Natalia sarcastically replied, but the call had already disconnected.

Daniel strutted into the room. He was impeccably dressed in a suit that she was sure he couldn't afford until his first paycheck from MBI hit his account. She smiled as he walked by, enjoying his newfound confidence.

"Who was that?" Daniel queried.

"Well," Natalia began to answer, "thanks to you, I was offered a job as an assistant for Bunny Vladigan. That was her. She is picking me up downstairs."

Daniel stopped in his tracks, visibly confused. He stood up straight and turned around to look at Natalia. "Really?" he asked. Two little lines formed between his eyes, looking like he was trying to work out how that happened.

"Yeah. I ran into her the other day, and she remembered us from the club. We talked about your new job and my joblessness, and she said she needed a new assistant. I wanted to surprise you with dinner tonight to thank you, but oh well. Surprise!"

His confusion, now wiped from his face, was replaced with a look of beaming pride. "Well, I am so happy for you. I'm thrilled I created an opportunity for you, but I am sure you earned it all alone."

The irony was not lost on Natalia as she stood up and stretched.

Daniel grabbed his briefcase, phone, and keys and reached for the door.

"Oh, um..." Daniel began, letting go of the door handle but not looking away. He ran his foot along the baseboard and muttered, "Would you mind cleaning up your things today? If you have the time after work, of course. If you can..."

"I've been keeping all of my things in my closet," Natalia stated, looking at him with her big, puppy dog eyes as he finally turned to look at her.

"Natalia, that is not a closet. You are just draping your clothes over my armchair, storing your shoes underneath, and leaving your cosmetics on the windowsill," he blurted out before he knew what he was doing. He quickly turned his gaze back to the door in disbelief at his brief outburst.

She shifted her weight and gave him a teasing smile when he turned back toward her. "Don't worry, Daniel. I'll get this place all cleaned up before you get home." She stomped her feet together abruptly, straightening up rigidly, and mocked a salute.

Daniel blushed to a deep red, said goodbye, and made his way out of the door. Natalia dropped her salute and flopped back onto the couch.

Bunny had to be downstairs already, she thought. *What did she want? Did she know Natalia had drinks with Stuart yesterday?*

What does someone wear not knowing if they are going to breakfast, on an errand, or getting dumped in the river?

"Ugh," she sighed loudly, dramatically rolling herself off the couch onto her hands and knees and crawling over to her makeshift closet.

***

On her way down to the lobby, Natalia thought again about Bunny's intentions. She earnestly hoped Bunny didn't intend for her to do real administrative work. That would be an uncomfortable conversation, indeed.

She remembered a girl she had always wanted to be friends with in middle school. Her name was Jodie. Natalia would be invited to a birthday party of Jodie's and would look forward to it for weeks. However, when she arrived, it was abundantly clear that her mother invited the entire class, whether Jodie wanted them there or not. Natalia was one of the latter.

Whatever she said would earn her an eye roll from Jodie. Whatever she did would result in a loud tongue click and Jodie bending over and whispering to a friend behind her hand. As an adult, Natalia could easily classify Jodie as a bully. She walked around school like everyone was beneath her and always had a lollypop in her mouth. For years, Natalia begged her mom for lollypops because, to Natalia, they were cool. Because no matter how mean Jodie was, how many people she turned against her, and how sick the rumors were that she started, Natalia wanted Jodie's approval. Natalia was sure that Jodie, now an adult, would deny being a bully since there was no physical harm. But the effects of her cruel words, demeaning stares, and silent judgment crushed Natalia's spirit and confidence nearly as much as her mother did. Was Stuart forcing Bunny to entertain Natalia? Was this like getting invited by a popular girl's parent? Bunny was friendly when they met at the apartment, but Natalia was unsure of the situation. Was she going to spend the day with this woman who would roll her eyes and click her tongue at everything Natalia said? As Natalia waltzed through the lobby, she shook off the Jodie jitters—her name for it when she assumed someone would be a bitch because of some slight similarity to Jodie. In Bunny's case, there were no similarities besides the fact that Natalia, for some reason, really wanted her approval. As well as Stuart's.

She had opted for a pair of tight black jeans, a spaghetti-strapped sequined top, stilettos, and an oversized sweater that hung over her arm in case they were to be outdoors. When she stepped out onto the sidewalk, she found a stretch limousine parked at the curb, with a rear door held open by a breathtakingly handsome man with deep ebony skin, wearing a sharp-looking suit.

"Good morning, Ms. Zapakh," the hottie said in a deep voice with a Central African accent.

"Hel-lo," she purred back at him in two distinct syllables with an added wink as she slid into the car. She kept her eyes on him until he closed the door. A chill ran up her spine as she compared her flirty tease to the way her mother would talk to men. Shaking off the disturbing thought, she glanced over to Bunny who was riding backward with her seat backed against the driver's.

"He's something, isn't he?" Bunny said, clearly knowing the answer. "His name is Diambu. He doesn't say much, but he's certainly nice to look at. You won't be surprised to know he is a model. He drives for me when he isn't at a shoot."

Natalia just stared at the back of Diambu's head, making a mental note to run an image search on him later to find some photos of him without the suit.

Turning back to Bunny, Natalia tried to get comfortable but unconsciously continued to fidget with the minibar door. Open, close. Open, close. She stared at Bunny, who sat in the center of the luxurious, soft, leather bench seat, with her platinum hair piled high upon her head, a tight, full-length, yet casual dress, and a small, pink fur draped over her shoulders. Her feet were crossed at the ankles, most likely because there was no room for give in the dress to allow her to cross her legs fully.

When she couldn't stand the silence, Natalia snapped, "Where are we going, Bunny?"

Bunny smiled the kind of half mouth smile that could be interpreted as playful, flirty, or dangerous. Natalia wasn't the slightest bit scared but was curious, indeed.

"Just out, my dear," Bunny said, reaching over to the bar opposite the alcohol and passing Natalia a cup of coffee. "Haven't you ever had a friend swing by with coffee and take you shopping?"

"Uh, no," Natalia answered, still skeptical and unsure if Bunny was teasing. "Is that a real thing people do?"

Bunny laughed heartily, then unrolled the divider window so she could talk to the driver.

"Diambu, dear. Take us to the spa. I think we need a day of relaxation and bonding."

ELVIS HAS LEFT THE BUILDING

The notification appeared on Natalia's phone, letting her know that her new mark, Betty, had left her apartment. She would be heading down the elevator from her lush condo, which was at least partly paid for with the hefty pension she was receiving from MBI. Natalia watched the second hand on her watch for forty-three seconds, then pressed the down button for the elevator just one floor below. Over the last week, Natalia had timed Betty, and it took her between forty and forty-five seconds to close her apartment door and walk down the hall to the elevator. Natalia positioned herself on the sixth floor of Betty's apartment building and timed the elevator just right so she could ride down with the old lady. Fortunately, this building was not as extravagant as Stuart and Bunny's. The top floor here did not have its own private elevator. The top contained four condos rather than just one, so Natalia did have to deal with the possible wild card of having one of Betty's neighbors ride down with them.

The light above the elevator illuminated in time with a delicate *ding*, then the doors opened. Natalia was pleased to see that Betty was alone unless you count her two little yip-yip dogs. Both dogs were small; their hair was smooth and combed, and even in a few places, looked as if they had been curled with curlers. The little fluff-balls had giant bows atop their heads, pulling the long hair off their faces and exposing their flat noses and large bulbous eyes.

Natalia stepped into the elevator, grabbed the railing, and pulled her right heel up to her hip to stretch her quads. She was dressed in running clothes since it was morning, and she wanted an excuse to leave the building and follow the same route as Betty.

"Good morning," Betty said cordially, in a proper yet shaky voice.

Natalia pulled one of her earbuds from her ear and replied, "Good morning." With her hands on her knees, she crouched down and said, "Cute dogs. What are their names?"

Betty bent over and picked up the cream-colored one with reddish eye drainage running down its face. She held the dog close to her cheek, raised one of its paws with her hand, and in a baby voice said, "I'm Priscilla. Aren't I so cute?"

Natalia did not like dogs, so she had to up her acting game. She forced a smile and tried not to cringe when the woman picked up her other dog and with a deep voice, said, "I'm Elvis. I'm a hunk of burning love."

What the actual fuck? Natalia thought to herself. It was bad enough that this woman needed to make voices for her dogs, but she had dressed this poor male dog in a big white, sequined bow.

"Cute," Natalia said through gritted teeth.

"Priscilla and Elvis," she repeated with a fake laugh.

"They're litter mates."

Ewww. Gross.

Thankfully, the elevator doors opened. Natalia motioned with her arm out for the lady and her furry companions to exit while she held down the "door open" button.

Still holding Elvis, Betty grabbed his paw and waved, saying in a deep voice, "Thank you. Thank you very much," as they exited.

Natalia took a deep breath to squash down her aggravation when she smelled something off. Not a smell of a person, personality, or feeling, but something sour that makes your nose hairs curl up. She glanced to the back of the elevator as she stepped off to see a small yellow puddle. A man was walking onto the elevator as she was walking off, and he gave her a disgusted look after seeing the pee on the floor.

"Don't look at me," she said defensively, following Betty as she, Pricilla, and Elvis left the building.

Natalia stayed close to half a block behind Betty and her dogs, attempting to look natural by bending over to stretch or checking her phone when they made their incomprehensibly frequent stops to sniff almost everything. The more irritated she was by this woman, the more she looked forward to ridding the planet of her.

Her hand instinctively reached down to her hip pack, where she had a full syringe of pure, liquid oxycodone. Through Natalia's review of the data Bunny relayed to her from Stuart's program, she learned that Betty had hip surgery six months ago, which explained the slow pace of her walk and caused her to form a nice little opioid addiction. Natalia picked up her speed as the crowds thinned out by the little corner park where Betty took her dogs.

Natalia stopped dead in her tracks as she watched Pricilla, who just took a piss in the elevator, take a Doberman-sized dump on the sidewalk, all while Betty walked on, oblivious.

She just left her dog's shit there for anyone to step on?

Natalia grew excited to eliminate the rude woman with her unacceptable pet owner behavior.

She spoke up from behind, saying, "Hello, again," then jogged right next to Betty and pulled her into a tight embrace while she stuck the syringe in her neck.

"Good to see you," she said in a normal tone, then in a whisper, said, "You forgot to pick up Priscilla's poop."

Betty just stood and stared straight ahead when Natalia let her go and jogged off in the other direction. She had spent hours crushing Betty's pills to a powder so fine that they could be injected into the bloodstream faster. Natalia had hoped the woman wouldn't collapse in her arms but hold on a few minutes past when she ran off.

Natalia was nearly a block away when she heard a man yell, "Call an ambulance!"

Another voice hollered, "She is holding dog treats. Did she have dogs?"

Natalia ran on, pleased with her work, but feeling a tug in her gut to turn around and help find the dogs. She tried to ignore the unfamiliar sensation and stopped, pulling out her phone. Her fingers raced over the buttons as she deleted Betty's name from her contacts.

As hard as she tried to fight the guilt of possibly subjecting the dogs to the same fate as their owner, she turned to head back. Natalia consciously fixed her face into the look of concern for the woman who was currently surrounded by a crowd. Fortunately, she was concerned for the dogs and with the group around Betty only growing in size, she didn't feel the need to pretend to help.

Keeping her head on a swivel, Natalia kept a look out for the dogs. They shouldn't be hard to find the with the big-ass bows on top of their heads.

The park to her right was small but clean. Being only two lots in size, the paths and grass were designed to make it look bigger. A small, colorful playground sat in the far corner, backing up to the fence of the adjoining properly. Had the dogs run into the road, it would've been quickly noticed by onlookers. The park was more appealing.

Goosebumps rose on Natalia's arms and she froze in place. Suddenly feeling self conscious, she wrapped her arms around herself and looked around once more. Someone was watching her. Had someone seen her inject Betty with the lethal dose? Was someone following her?

As Natalia turned around to face the end of a barrier hedge, she found two bulging eyeballs staring back at her, unblinking with concentration and drive. At some point during their escape, Pricilla must have lost her bow, because her long hair atop her head fell over her eyes while Elvis pounded her from behind.

A pitter patter of quick steps came from behind her, followed by a voice.

"Mommy, look at these cute doggies. This one is getting a piggy-back ride," the child yelled with glee.

With disgust replacing her feelings of guilt, in addition to the fact that the child and her mother appeared to be helping the lost dogs, Natalia took off to finish her jog and wash the incest from her eyeballs.

NEW DIGS

Daniel was pleased to find that he had beaten Natalia home from work. He had exciting news for her and wanted to celebrate. She had been patient and supportive of him and slept on his couch without complaint for over a month.

After changing into jeans and a t-shirt, he wandered into the kitchen and browsed the cupboard for something he could use to make the two of them cocktails. He was disappointed to find the shelves close to bare, except for a box of Ritz crackers and an old bottle of schnapps. He stepped over to the refrigerator to find it equally sparse. After some serious scavenging, Daniel was staring at his counter, where he lined up crackers, Prosecco, schnapps, cream cheese, strawberry jelly, and raspberries.

While he tried to assemble something palatable, he remembered the cocktail hour his parents had every day when he was young. From 3:30 to 5:30 p.m. every afternoon, his parents would sit in their lounge, sip cocktails, snack on elaborately made appetizers, and chat about their day. Daniel was never allowed into the lounge during cocktail hour, but he would sit on the floor outside the door to the room and listen. It was funny to him, thinking back to how his mother was always exhausted by 3:30 p.m. and would complain about her long day. Daniel was sure the most tiring thing she ever did was walk down the stairs from her room. She had the help pick out clothes, clean the house, cook the meals, drive her places, in addition to a full rotation of nannies to take care of him. His mother liked to let guests assume that she made the drinks and appetizers, and his father went along with it, not to cause a stir. In reality, she didn't lift a finger.

A few minutes later, Daniel stared down at his arrangement. He poured two glasses of Prosecco with a splash of schnapps and added a raspberry and mint leaf garnish. Daniel was also proud of the plate he assembled with crackers topped with cream cheese and a tiny blob of strawberry jelly.

It wasn't much, and he needed to get to the store, but he wanted to make Natalia happy. Things had turned around since he met her. He heard the keys in the door and stood behind the counter, smiling as Natalia walked in.

"What are you smiling at?" she asked playfully. "You look happy or guilty... or both, like a dog that ate something off the table."

Daniel walked over and handed her a drink. "I have some exciting news. Come sit," he said, gesturing to the barstools by the counter.

"Oh, thank you, I am starving," she said, grabbing one of the crackers with cream cheese. "These are cute," she said, taking a bite. When she finished chewing, she continued, "And delicious! I'm impressed. So, what is your news?"

"Well, I was talking with Stuart today, and he said one of the people in his building will be living in Prague for a year and needs to rent their condo. It is on one of the lower levels, which I don't care about, but Stuart was very apologetic... I guess he's at the top. It has two bedrooms, so it would be perfect for us. What do you think?" He felt nervous since he had already told Stuart he wanted it. He knew he should've talked to Natalia first. What if she didn't want to move?

She looked at him over the top of her drink with a stoic look. He was getting more nervous as the seconds ticked by. There was no way he could afford the rent on his own. Unbeknownst to Daniel, Natalia had convinced Stuart to agree to partially pay for the condo. Natalia was in a unique situation where she could demand pretty much anything from the guy. But he was growing on her, and she didn't want to overreach.

Finally, she cracked a smile. "That sounds amazing, Daniel! How soon can we move in? I can get my *closet* packed up pretty quickly!" Natalia laughed a single-syllable hearty laugh at herself.

"Whenever we're ready. Stuart also told me how much Bunny has enjoyed working with you. She said you're a very hard worker, good with direction, and amazing with people."

Natalia coughed, and some of her drink sprayed from her nose and mouth.

"Are you okay?" Daniel asked, handing her a paper towel.

"Yes. Thank you. It just went down the wrong pipe." Natalia recovered and raised her glass.

"To our new place!" Daniel said, holding up his glass.

Natalia smiled and gently touched her glass to his. "New place, new jobs, new life!"

And they clinked glasses.

FIRE IN THE HOLE

Natalia had been looking for an excuse to take a vacation. Growing up, her mom would have weeks of bliss, talking about how Natalia's dad had made plans to take the three of them on vacation. She planned activities, bought new clothes, and dreamt of breath-taking days on the beach and romantic nights in a bungalow on the water. Then, without fail, something would come up… he had a meeting he could not miss, he was mugged, or his wife had a breakdown… nothing worth canceling over in Tatiana's mind, but it happened.

Weeks of depression would follow. She would shut herself in her room and leave Natalia to fend for herself. She would knock and talk through the closed door every so often, hoping to pull her mom out of her funk.

"Mom? I won the science fair today."

No answer.

"Mom? At least you got all those cool new clothes and bags out of it."

No answer.

"Mom? I made a new dinner recipe."

No answer.

"Mom? Look on the bright side. At least his wife had a breakdown."

No answer.

But, like clockwork, Tatiana would emerge two weeks later and refuse to talk about the canceled plans, her disappointment, or the man that caused them both. But, like a moth to a flame, he would return, and she would fall in love again.

It only took a few times for Natalia to stop believing these trips would ever happen, but her mom was a sucker and fell for it hook, line, and sinker every time.

Things for Natalia were different as an adult and on her own, but she was still very skeptical. She didn't believe it when Bunny presented her with a round-trip, first-class ticket to Hawaii. She didn't think the trip would happen even when they went shopping for vacation clothes. She didn't believe she would leave New York even when she sat on her flight and graciously accepted a cocktail and warm towel from the flight attendant. But after thirteen hours of watching the man in the seat next to her drift in and out of sleep, she feared his dramatic head nods would cause his head to roll off his neck and down the aisle; Natalia was in Maui, actually on vacation. Technically, it was business, but she was somewhere she had always wanted to go.

The lights in the cabin came on, and the flight attendant rattled off the gates of connecting flights and baggage claim directions. Natalia stood, grabbed her bag, and looked over at her row mate, who finally looked to have fallen into a deep sleep in a new position that kept his head attached. She thought of waking him, but instead, she spit her gum into his lap, put on her hat and sunglasses, and walked off the plane.

***

Natalia knew that her mark, Janice Ledbetter, was planning to stay five days, so she had plenty of time to devise a plan. They were staying at the same resort, which meant plenty of opportunity. Janice flew in from Florida late the night before. After arriving at the resort, Natalia wanted to change into her swimsuit and fall asleep poolside until dinner.

Unlike her head-bobbing, drooling, elbow rest-hogging neighbor on the airplane, she had been unable to get any sleep on the flight.

As she checked into the hotel, Natalia couldn't help but overhear the raucous man pushing time shares behind her in the main section of the lobby.

"A Maui timeshare is an investment you will never regret. Your family will be able to use it for years to come. I would love to sign you up for our presentation. We will provide you and your husband with a full dinner in any of our resort restaurants on us, just for attending," the man aggressively pushed.

"Oh, it's just me. My husband passed away last spring," a woman's voice replied.

"Oh, gosh, I am so sorry for assuming. Would you like to sign up for our presentation later this afternoon so you can treat yourself to a nice dinner on us for attending?"

"No, thank you. I plan to bike down the volcano in the morning, and I heard we have to leave the hotel at 2:00 a.m. to get there by sunrise. I think I will head to bed early tonight," the woman explained.

"Well, in that case, I'll sign you up for tomorrow afternoon. Name, please?"

"Janice. Janice Ledbetter"

Natalia whipped around to observe the conversation behind her.

"Here is your room key. Enjoy your stay," said the woman behind the counter, bringing Natalia's attention back to the matter at hand.

"Thank you," she said, taking the key card and strolling by the timeshare booth.

What a stroke of luck. Natalia hadn't planned to get started so early, but she already had a head start on her mission, having located the soon-to-be victim by chance.

Natalia stood at the elevator bank staring blankly at the closed doors, pondering the new information she now had. After catching a quick but good look at the woman, Natalia noted that she was short, maybe five feet tall, with a shock of white hair cut in a bob. She was petite to the extent of looking frail. It was hard to believe anyone who looked that slight and fragile would even attempt to climb onto a bike out of fear of breaking a hip or two. Biking down a volcano sounded pretty extreme for a little old lady. She needed to find out more.

Natalia abruptly turned away from the elevator and almost ran into a couple presumably heading to their room.

"Woah, little lady!" the man exclaimed.

"Excuse me," Natalia said quietly, her mind still elsewhere.

"Excuse you?" the man laughed as he waved his hand in front of his nose, then coughed after his wife elbowed him in the ribs.

"Sorry," the woman muttered, clearly embarrassed. "Excuse us," she added, dragging her bag and her husband into the now-open elevator.

Natalia had her eyes on the concierge her entire walk down the hallway. She knew what she had to do. She needed to get on that volcano bike ride, and then she could relax. When she almost arrived at the concierge stand, the timeshare guy stepped in her path.

"Would you like a free dinner?"

"No," Natalia answered abruptly as she altered her path to walk around the annoying salesman.

***

Less than an hour later, Natalia was finally heading to her room. The bike trip down a volcano turned out to be considerably less extreme than she had envisioned. The guides drive the group up to the top of a now-dormant volcano—which takes most of the fear factor out of the equation—with plans to arrive just before sunrise. The group stands at the top, taking pictures and watching the sunrise before coasting down the road. With the slope of the mountain, little to no pedaling would be necessary. The image she had painted in her head of a little old lady riding a BMX bike down a rocky mountain trailed by lava was clearly a misconception. Still pretty ballsy for an elderly lady, however. The concierge told her the ride down was nearly two hours long and that they stopped halfway for a snack and a drink. He also mentioned that even though it was a gorgeous eighty-two degrees out, it was pretty chilly at the top of the volcano before the sun rose, so to dress warmly. Natalia didn't pack anything warm, so she stopped at the gift shop and bought the tackiest sweatshirt she could find on her way up to her room.

The hoodie was navy blue with a scantily clad woman on the front saying, *"Wish You Were Her* above *Maui, HI."*

After keying into her room, she tossed her bag in the closet, used the bathroom, then fell face-first onto her bed, planning to rest her eyes for just a few minutes before hitting the pool.

***

Natalia woke with a start when she heard the old-school, rotary phone ring of the hotel room telephone. It took a few seconds to get her bearings, then she reached over and grabbed the phone while wiping drool from her chin.

"Hello?"

"Good morning. This is a wake-up call for your Volcano Bike Adventure. Please meet us downstairs in the lobby in fifteen minutes."

Natalia hung up the phone. *So much for an afternoon at the pool,* she thought to herself. She couldn't believe she had slept all afternoon and through dinner. She was getting ready to sit in a van and then ride down a mountain with Janice, and she had nothing planned. Natalia splashed water on her face, used the bathroom, re-applied deodorant, and threw on her new sweatshirt over the t-shirt and shorts she wore on the flight. She was sure she smelled ripe, but maybe that would keep people from trying to make small talk with her.

***

Most of the van ride up the volcano was uneventful. Six drowsy passengers climbed into the van with two guides sitting up front. The sky was pitch dark, with only a sliver of the moon for light.

For the first hour of the ride, the only noise that could be heard was the sound of the tires humming on the pavement and the occasional snore of a passenger who had dozed off. Natalia wondered how anyone could sleep in the uncomfortable bench seats with Janice's extremely potent perfume.

If this lady had a scent, Natalia would never be able to smell it through the perfume cloud that sucked the oxygen out of her lungs.

The guides shared local information and trivia when the vacationers began to stir. The driver, who asked to be called Uncle Earl, talked about how many miles they would be riding, twenty-six, and the unique vegetation they would see, like The Maui Silversword. He name-dropped some famous celebrities he met in his line of work and told the story of how he arrived in Hawaii on vacation eighteen years ago and never left.

A man Natalia recognized from the elevator the previous day chimed in, "Is it true what they say about the altitude?"

Deborah, the female guide in the passenger seat, replied, "We will travel up to over ten thousand feet above sea level. Some of you will notice the thinner air, while others will not. Sit down if you feel faint or dizzy, and it will pass."

"Not that," the elevator guy quickly cut in with a jovial smile. "I hear that your bowels can unexpectedly and powerfully release at high altitudes," he added with a snicker.

"I have heard that's happened to some people. But to be honest, I think it has more to do with the time of day we arrive at the top," Janice piped up for the first time on the ride.

Natalia cringed. She didn't mind the poop talk so much as the fact Janice said *To Be Honest*. She hated that phrase. Why would someone say that? Should she infer that the woman is not being honest the rest of the time?

"Well, I hope the facilities are zoned for horses because I am ready to blow, and we are not even up to the top altitude yet!"

"There will be porta-potties at the top of Haleakala that you can use, though it can prove difficult as the sun will not yet be up."

"Truth be told, I would prefer to tinkle on the side of the road," Janice interjected again.

Natalia's hands curled into fists in her hoodie's front pocket. She started to pick at her thumb cuticles with her middle finger nail, digging and picking nervously. With every chunk of skin she removed, she winced in pain and thought about the joy she would receive, knocking this *honest, tinkling* woman off her bike.

"I'm not talking about number one, lady. Oomph," the man said, grunting as he took another elbow to the ribs.

***

When the group arrived at the Haleakala National Park, everyone piled out with grunts and groans, stretching their legs and taking deep breaths of the clean, thin air. A young couple made their way over to a porta-potty to the right of the parked van. Another couple helped the guides unload the gear. They all needed to put on full wind suits that the tour company provided. Natalia pretended to stretch when Janice walked up to her.

"No offense, but a nice young lady like yourself should be embarrassed to wear a sweatshirt like that," she said. Then she turned to walk toward the groupings of potties slightly up the hill.

"None taken," Natalia called after her with a smile.

She noticed more vans were driving up the volcano at a distance. The van she rode up in appeared to be the first tour group to make it to the top, but there would be a bigger crowd soon. She may be able to separate herself and Janice from her group, but how many others will be doing the same ride?

"Too many potential witnesses are on the way up; time for plan B," she muttered, quietly following Janice into the dark.

Fully aware of how flimsy the locks on the porta-potty doors were, Natalia approached the plastic box in the deep darkness and pulled hard on the door, which despite being locked with the occupied sign displayed, sprung open. The sudden movement caused Janice to stand from her squatting position, stunned. Natalia could barely see her face in the darkness, but catching the sliver of the moon's reflection in Janice's glasses was enough to reach for her throat as the door slammed shut behind her. Gone was the overpowering perfume smell, now replaced with the pungent smell of high-altitude shit. With her right hand solidly gripping Janice's throat to keep her from making noise, her left hand reached behind her back and locked the door. She turned her attention back to Janice and said, "You're like a chicken. Not just your scrawny, little neck, but with the way your eyes popped out when I opened the door." She laughed, wishing she could get a better view, but the darkness was all-encompassing.

Natalia knew she could snap Janice's neck with little to no effort, but the space was so small, and she didn't want to bump into the walls of the porta-potty. She felt around with her left hand and made contact with a ledge on the side of the wall. It was likely meant for holding cell phones or keys, but it felt like it was something that would hold a bar of soap in a hotel bathroom, down to the little bumps to let the water drain.

Still staring in the direction of the ledge, she exclaimed in a British accent, "I now dub thee, Neck Breaker," and with her right hand still gripping the front of Janice's throat, she slammed the base of her neck into the hard molded plastic, shattering both the ledge and Janice's chicken neck.

She could hear the rock-crunching of the tires on the other vans pulling into the parking lot and wondered how she would get out *and* lock the door from the outside when the obvious struck her. She lifted the toilet seat, revealing a much larger hole beneath, and unceremoniously dumped Janice headfirst into the base underneath. The frail and lightweight body made very little noise when she hit bottom, thanks to the "soft solids" already down there.

As she reached for the door, she thought it would be a good idea to "tinkle" before the long bike ride down the hill, so she placed the toilet seat back down, sat, and sighed, relieving herself. It was a long and forceful pee after the two-hour van ride.

When she stood back up, she gave herself a squirt of hand sanitizer she found while groping the interior walls and opened the door to the approaching and very eager man from the van awkwardly running toward her. He appeared to be clenching his butt cheeks so hard that he waddled when he ran.

"Whew, just in time. I'm about to drop bombs!"

Natalia was walking away when she heard the porta-potty door slam shut, and the man inside yelled, "Fire in the hole!"

crunching ice cubes

After returning from Hawaii, Natalia felt the need to be *un*-surrounded by nature. Her previous urge to leave the city, get back to nature, and be alone had transformed into an intense need to walk the busy streets of Manhattan at rush hour. She missed the aggressive sounds of horns honking and people hurling curse words at each other. She missed the artificial light and cell towers designed to look like indigenous trees. She missed the smells of the random, greenish smoke floating out of the sewer, the freshly pissed upon walls, and the waterlogged, red hot dogs. Maybe the first two smells are more nostalgic than something she missed, but she really did miss those artificial hot dogs.

She walked down the street, smiling and completely unbothered as people bounced off her like an old-school game of Pong. One person bumped into her so hard she had to brace herself to keep from hitting a building exterior. Her hand touched something warm and sticky, and she instinctively pulled her hand back and sniffed her fingers. More disgusted with herself than whatever the hell she had just touched, she wiped her palms down the front of her faded blue jeans, leaving an odd brownish tint. A homeless man jumped out onto the sidewalk, causing the foot traffic to redirect in a wide berth around him. He was yelling at a group of people standing on the corner. They appeared to be tourists by the sheer number of photographs they were taking. A few of the younger people in the crowd were overdressed like they thought visiting New York City required red carpet attire. Or maybe they were dressed to party, just in case some bodega had a backdoor that led to a private party. She wondered how they were managing to walk over the grates on the sidewalk in their high heels. The rest of the group was dressed purely for comfort and walking. They donned matching warm-up suits, hats, and "I LOVE NY" scarves. It was an odd group, but despite the differences in their dress, they seemed to be having a good time.

The homeless man continued to yell, "God damn tourists. I can smell you. You stink!"

At first, Natalia laughed, thinking of the irony of a man who smelled like his own piss could say these people smelled. But then she wondered if this odd man could smell things the way she could.

When she approached him, he stopped yelling temporarily and said, "They stink. Can you smell them? I know you're not a tourist because you don't stink. They stink!"

She decided not to engage the man and to be happy that he didn't group her with the stinky tourists. As she walked away, past the crowd and down the street, she wondered if the way she could smell anxiety, fear, and disgust, if that man could smell where people were from. The idea seemed silly, but she supposed her smelling skills would be curious to most people as well.

She picked up her pace, craving a good ol' street hot dog more than ever. She turned the corner, prepared to see Tyrone, her usual random-meat-parts vendor. To her surprise, instead of Tyrone, who was a very tall and lanky teenager with an amazing sense of humor, was a short, fat, balding, white dude. She didn't know if he was old or just bald. His face looked rather young, but the tufts of hair over his ears were wiry and grey.

He must have noticed her staring because he looked at her and, in the most New Yorker fashion, held up his hands, palms up, and shouted, "Hey lady, you want a hot dog, or what?"

While waiting for an answer, he tipped his tall, white, Styrofoam cup upwards and filled his mouth full of ice cubes.

"Where's Tyrone?" she asked while trying to ignore the little, cylindrical crystals as they fell down his chin and rested on his large, protruding belly.

"He's off today. What do you want?" he asked as several ice chips flew from his lips.

She didn't answer right away but watched as his open mouth chewed his ice and occasionally smacked his lips, sucking his discolored upper teeth with his tongue.

"I think I'll have..." Natalia started but stopped again when she saw that he tipped his cup back for another helping of ice.

"Yeah? Continue," he said, mostly inaudibly, but with an accompanying rotating hand gesture making what he was saying more obvious.

"Can you even *hear* my order when you're chewing like that?"

"I chew ice to keep me from eating," he said, patting his belly. "The boss says that eating on the job is a disgusting habit. Plus, it helps me lose weight."

"Really?" she said, feigning belief, looking him up and down. "Okay, I'll have one red hot, please."

"One red hot, coming up!" he yelled as if he was about to perform an amazing trick for everyone within earshot.

The street vendor tipped his cup back and continued to chew, mouth agape while prepping her order. She watched as he pulled a bun out of the warmer, then just before he placed the beautiful, red goodness on the bun, a chunk of ice flew out of his mouth and landed between the bun and the hot dog.

"You want mustard?" he asked, causing another piece of ice to land on Natalia's chest. "Oops. Sorry, lady. You want me to get that?" He gave her a disgusting, rotten-teeth smile and held her hot dog out for her to take.

She stared down at the skinny, pink hot dog she had been looking forward to eating, now covered in small ice chunks, and was reminded of the skinny, old man she had to kill last week in his bathroom with his pants still around his ankles. She only justified his death because of his annoying sneezes. Some people sneeze once. Some sneezes come in threes. But this guy would sneeze five to ten times in a row.

She looked up at the street vendor, leaned over, and whispered, "I've killed people for much less."

Then, leaving the hot dog behind, abruptly turned, rounded the corner, and headed back home.

DINNER AND DRUGS

Natalia and Bunny were at the spa for the fourth week in a row. They thought it was a good idea to meet regularly and establish a working relationship, and as Bunny says, "A girl can only shop so much."

The two had just finished their ninety-minute massages and were soaking in a hot tub. In a very short period of time, they had become quite comfortable with each other. Natalia was hardly modest but would never think of walking around a locker room unclothed. However, being with Bunny was what Natalia always thought it would be like to be with a sister. She never felt insecure, judged, or shy, even with Bunny's centerfold body on display right next to her.

She compared their being naked together in the hot tub or showers to what contestants are like on the show where they are left naked in the woods for weeks at a time. They probably check each other out for the first hour, but then the novelty wears off, and they are just two people covered in dirt, bug bites, and feces. Fortunately, the two ladies were clean and bite-free.

They sat opposite each other, Bunny with her arms stretched out along the side of the hot tub with her breasts poking up and saying hello to the world, and Natalia slumped way down, with her arms by her sides, and the warm, iridescent bubbles covering her up to her chin. They both had their eyes closed and were enjoying each other's company in silence until Natalia questioned Bunny.

"Hey, Bunny. If I need something I wouldn't likely find in a store, how do you propose I get it?"

Bunny didn't move, kept her eyes closed, and replied, "Francisco can help you get anything you need."

Francisco was Bunny's masseuse. When they arrived at the spa hours ago, Natalia was angry with Bunny when she saw who would be giving them their spa treatment. Bunny went with the beautiful Latin God, Francisco, whom Natalia recognized from that first night they met at the club. While she begrudgingly followed Brynhildr, a huge woman with a strong German accent and five o'clock shadow. Fortunately, Brynhildr, though not all that much to look at, was firm yet gentle and very good with her fingers.

Francisco entered the private tub room with tall glasses of sparkling water and cocktails as if on cue. All he needed was a fan and some grapes, and Natalia's fantasy would be complete.

"Francisco, would you mind helping Natalia acquire some items she needs?" Bunny asked, having not even opened her eyes to grab her drink.

"Of course," Francisco replied. "In fact, I'll be leaving here soon if you want to discuss your needs over lunch or coffee?"

Natalia hesitated. She was unsure whether Bunny understood what she was asking. Her quick and unfettered reply made it seem like she may be under the impression that Natalia needed someone to take in her dry cleaning or to detail her car. And, still unsure of the nature of Bunny and Francisco's relationship, Natalia glanced uncomfortably back and forth between the two reading the room for tension.

Francisco noticed her pause and uneasiness and added, "Or, you can just tell me what you need when you leave, and I can handle it for you." He looked down at his feet. "We don't have to do lunch or anything."

Natalia realized that she had hurt his feelings. "Oh, no. I'm so sorry. I was just wondering if there is a misunderstanding. I am not entirely sure that you can do what I need. Not do. I mean, get," she said, trying to get her words out as fast as she could, but stumbled until she added, "I would love to have lunch with you."

***

Natalia sat at a table in the corner by the window in a restaurant not too far from the spa. She watched as Francisco made his way to the table from the bar, where he stopped to chat with the waitstaff and bartenders he apparently knew.

The first time Natalia set eyes on Francisco, he was sitting next to Bunny, and even though Natalia liked men, no one else was visible when they were with Bunny. All eyes are on her, her beauty, and her amazing boobs.

The second time she saw him was in the spa. She wasn't as much checking him out as thinking of how she got short-changed when she was matched up with the hefty German lady.

She did remember when he walked in with their drinks, however. To her surprise, he came in barefoot. His feet were surprisingly not disgusting. She never considered feet anything but a way to get around, but for a moment, she thought of Francisco's feet as sexy. She was impressed with his professional demeanor when he walked into a private room with two nude women in a hot tub, one of them with her breasts floating on top of the water like beach balls. He seemed not the slightest bit flustered and was a complete gentleman. She thought him likely gay, which would explain why Stuart didn't seem to mind the amount of time Bunny spent with him.

Less than an hour later, Natalia watched how he moved and his mannerisms as he talked with his friends, and she got a full, non-creepy look at him.

He was beautiful. His light brown skin glowed against his bright white starched shirt. His thick, black hair hung limply over his forehead, clearly meant to look as though he woke up that way, but she was sure there was effort put into making it look so good. His deep brown eyes were rimmed with long black eyelashes and were beautifully contrasted by the flawless whites of his eyes. But, for the first time, she realized that it was his smile that completely sucked her in. His wide smile with bright, white teeth surrounded by plump, kissable lips. And to bring it all home, an adorable dimple on his right cheek.

"Natalia. Are you okay?" Francisco asked, his smile disappearing.

She hadn't noticed how hard she was staring at him until he sat at the table.

Maybe she was staring creepily after all. That smile. That smile that had just frozen her in time was meant for her.

"Yes. Sorry. I just feel like I am seeing you for the first time." She paused and looked down at her lap, wondering if she could ask him the question that was on her mind. When she drew her eyes back up to his, she asked, "I know it is not my business, but can I ask what the nature of your relationship is with Bunny? I would ask her, but I am afraid just asking could cost me my job."

Francisco blushed and cleared his throat. "When I was just out of high school, I began to head down a dark path. I was selling drugs in a back alley and got jumped and beaten within an inch of my life. Bunny and Stuart were the ones that found and got me to the hospital. For some reason, Bunny felt that she had to see my recovery through, and by the time I was discharged from the hospital, we had formed a unique friendship. I would say she is like a mother to me, but really she is like a cool aunt. She and Stuart insisted on paying my way through school so I could get my massage therapy license and helped me get a great job. I owe them my life, but I would still do anything for them even if I didn't. I have never, in my life, met anyone so open to people embracing who they were born to be.

"Why do you ask?" he added with a coy smile, then quickly changed the subject. He continued, "So. What is it that I can help you with?"

Natalia's feeling of immense relief and even excitement to learn that he and Bunny were not romantic quickly turned to dread as she realized she had no idea how to ask for what she needed. How does one ask for illegal drugs, weapons, or other items she would not likely be able to acquire on her own?

"Um. I am not sure..." she began and then paused.

"How about I start? In my family, you have two career options. You either work for my grandmother at one of the family restaurants, or you deal drugs. I followed my cousins down the wrong path. We're still good, but I'm not in deep like I was. They know I'm on the straight and narrow now. So, if you need a last-minute reservation at the hottest brunch spot in town or you need to get your hands on something that you wouldn't be able to just walk into a store and buy, I'm your guy. No waiting period, background checks, or prescriptions needed," he stated confidently with a dimple-popping smile.

FINDING FLAWS

Back in high school, when the frequency of Natalia's dad's visits diminished, the frequency of Tatiana's one-night stands with random men increased.

Each one was premeditated because she would rush Natalia through dinner and send her into her room, telling her she would be back soon and that Natalia was not to leave her room under any circumstances until given the all-clear the following morning. She even left her with a bucket and a roll of toilet paper in case the need to use the bathroom arose. Having to degrade herself to sit on a makeshift toilet was one of the few times Natalia was happy to not see her reflection in the painted over mirrors. She would intentionally not drink or eat anything in anticipation of avoiding the use of the bucket, but one could only hold it for so long. Natalia would throw on her headphones and crank up the volume on whatever video she was watching in hopes of drowning out the sounds she did not want to hear.

Most men were there one night and gone the next morning, and never seen again. But Tatiana never learned her lesson. The following morning, she would be giddy about the new man, but when he did not return or call, she would turn everything around as if she planned it that way.

"Don't settle," she would tell Natalia. "If you find something you don't like about a man, toss him to the curb. You won't likely change him, so don't waste your time."

She would then explain to Natalia, very specifically, what she didn't like about each man once she gave up on him. *His eyes were too close together. One nostril was larger than the other. His eyebrows were uneven. His voice was too high-pitched.* Most of these so-called flaws, Natalia doubted, really existed, or maybe they were grossly exaggerated like a caricature. It was amazing how good her mother was at finding everyone else's flaws. Not once did she ever look to herself for why these men left.

If there were ever a man who was crazy enough to want to stick around, Natalia made sure to scare them off as best she could. She received so little love and support from Tatiana as it was. The last thing she needed was some dude to compete with. The morning after a guy stayed a second night, Natalia would sneak out when she heard the coffee brewing and add a few squirts of eye drops to the coffee mug Tatiana reserved for her man of the day. The mug was small with a dainty handle, and her mother was convinced she could tell a lot about a man based on how he could handle the little mug. It didn't take long before John, Rick, Sam, or Tom ran for the door or the bathroom, too embarrassed to return an th ird time.

CLean up on AISLe FOUr

Natalia came to the realization that she never wanted to retire. Retirees didn't all spend their excess free time the same way, but the days were boring and filled with monotonous schedules as if they were just waiting for their lives to end. She had been following Margaret Humphrey for a few days now. Margaret was a tiny woman who looked like she would fly away if a slight breeze blew through. When Natalia followed her, she wondered things like... *Where does she buy her clothes? Does she have to shop in the kids' section? Can she wear adult shoes? Is she wearing adult shoes that are way too big?* Maybe that would explain the grating way she dragged her feet on the ground when she walked. She regularly wore outdoor slippers, but rather than pinch her toes to walk as people do in flip-flops, she dragged her feet one after the other at an excruciatingly slow pace.

Margaret shopped like the French. She woke for the day, drank a coffee, then walked a block to her neighborhood market, where she bought the food she needed for that day. This daily activity could fill up to three hours. Even with the store only a block away, Margaret walked so slowly that it could take her forty minutes in each direction. She would then spend well over an hour walking around and asking questions about produce freshness. Literally. Every. Damn. Day. Natalia hoped today would be the last time she would need to follow her. Margaret's daily schedule was so consistent Natalia couldn't imagine what else she could learn by following her any longer.

Rather than trail her from the apartment and waste precious time, Natalia waited for her on a bench outside the store. She checked her watch, wondering if she had somehow missed her, when she heard the unmistakable sound of Margaret's dragging feet against the concrete sidewalk in the distance. Schhhhhhhh. Schhhhhhhh. Schhhhhh. Thunk. Her shoe hit a crack in the sidewalk and fell off.

Crackle, crack. She bent over to flip her shoe over. "Ugh," she moaned as she stood back up. Schhh. Schhh. Schhh. She stuffed her foot back into the shoe. Schhhhhhhh. Schhhhhhhh. Schhhhhh.

It was agonizing to listen to. Over and over. Natalia wondered how the hell this woman had not tripped and fallen as many times as she lost a shoe by hitting a crack in the sidewalk. Surely one fall and every bone in this woman's frail body would shatter into small bits of dust and fly away in the breeze.

Natalia sat comfortably on the bench, taking the time to finish her coffee, knowing that even after five minutes, Margaret would still be just inside the door asking the Produce Manager what was fresh. The poor guy, probably in his late teens, was more of a stock boy. Natalia could tell he was a nice kid and tried to be kind to the sweet, old lady, but he didn't want to break her heart and tell her that by the time he unloaded the trucks, most of the produce had been picked, pulled, or cut a week ago or longer. Nothing was fresh. The seafood she asked about every day was previously frozen. The bread and pastries that looked like they had just popped out of the oven were shipped across the country and were so full of preservatives that they were likely to thank for Margaret's long life.

Natalia casually strolled into the store and examined some tomatoes while listening to Margaret badger the stock boy, over a peach she bought the previous day.

"You told me it was ripe, so I tried to eat it and almost broke a tooth."

"I'm sorry, ma'am. Would you like me to talk to a store manager about a refund or replacement?"

"No. I think a produce worker should know his fruits and when they are ripe. That peach should've sat on the windowsill for at least three more days. Are you even listening to me, boy?" Margaret snapped.

Sweet old lady, my ass, Natalia thought to herself. The way the angry woman treated the boy was the cherry on top. Natalia wouldn't have had a problem killing Margaret based on her feet dragging, both literal and figurative. But, adding her holier-than-thou attitude and rudeness made it all the easier.

Natalia heard the slow-motion shuffle of Margaret's feet start up again and knew she was on to bother someone in the deli. Natalia couldn't bear to listen to another conversation and cut over to the raw pasta section in the back, where she knew Margaret would end up.

Natalia turned the corner of the end cap to find an empty aisle and an industrial size bottle of clear hand soap. She couldn't imagine the store selling a bulk item of that size, so she deduced that an employee was likely planning to change out the soap in the bathrooms and got sidetracked. She glanced up and down the aisle one more time, checking for people or any cameras that may have been added since yesterday. When she was sure everything was clear, she dumped the entire bottle of soap on the ground.

She was amazed at how it seemed to level itself out over the floor, so it could only be seen if you were looking for it.

Natalia continued down to the end of the aisle and made her way into the next section, which looked like a weak attempt to diversify their offerings. There was a rack of coloring books, magazines, greeting cards, condoms, and perfume. It was so randomly organized that Natalia wondered if they were brought in by accident and just displayed all together. She smirked at the display of perfume and condoms together when she heard a crash in the next aisle, followed by someone running.

"Holy Shit!" the young, produce boy yelled in a way more adult voice than she imagined he could muster.

With that, Natalia made her way toward the front, grabbed a pack of gum and slid it into her pocket. She stood at the back of a crowd of onlookers, peaking her head between the shoulders of two teenage punks who snickered in their attempt to look concerned but who appeared to be just as entertained as Natalia. A loud thump echoed through the store as the produce boy slipped and fell on his way to help. A thin man dressed in stylish scrubs ran towards the chaos slower and more controlled than the produce boy but was met with the same fate none-the-less.

As much as Natalia wanted to watch the entertainment, she knew she needed to clear out before emergency workers arrived with questions. One last glance at the slippery slide of death left her with the last laugh. Produce boy gingerly moved to stand, only to fall once again; face first directly into the unmoving Margaret's crotch.

With all the chaos, she wondered in hindsight if she should've grabbed some food for dinner on her way out. She turned left to walk down the sidewalk, thankful not to have to listen to the sloshy, draggy feet all the way back, then glanced through the store window. The produce boy must have run to call an ambulance because Margaret lay alone, unmoving, in a very large pool of blood on the floor. Even outside the store, she was overwhelmed with the strong smell of cinnamon.

"Clean up in aisle four!" Natalia yelled and laughed as she made her way home, kicking herself for not grabbing a bottle or two of wine.

EGGPLANT DELIVERY

Natalia paced the apartment, waiting on a call or text from Francisco. He was so confident that he could get his hands on ricin that she initially had not a worry in the world. But, now that she was waiting on him, she began to wonder what kind of trance she was under to blindly trust those sexy dimples. Not totally blind since Bunny vouched for him, but still, it was not like Natalia to work with anyone else. The fewer people involved, the less chance of a screw-up. Scenario after scenario ran through her mind with each minute past his scheduled arrival time.

Did he strut up to some underground bunker and ask for poison?

Did the criminal chemist kidnap him or kill him and dump his body in Oyster Bay?

Did his family think he knew too much and force him to rejoin the mafia?

Was his mafia family just a front for undercover police work?

Was he going to show up with an entire SWAT team and arrest her?

She had been on edge already after a near miss last week. She had snuck into some old guy's house, planning to push him down the stairs. But, to her good fortune, the sight of her scared him so badly that he tripped and fell down the stairs on his own. So shocked at not having to do anything, she let her guard down and walked out of his apartment and right into a uniformed officer. Her heart stopped, and she couldn't swallow. She finally allowed herself to breathe when she looked down at his name tag and saw that he was an animal control worker who lived in the building. Why the hell did the animal control department model their uniforms after the NYPD, anyway?

She peaked out of her window, again checking to see if police cars were surrounding the building when a knock at the door came.

"AAAAHHH!" she screamed, dropping the curtains and whipping around in fright. She took a deep breath and walked quietly over to the door. Not sure why she was tip-toeing since she had just screamed at the top of her lungs. She placed her hand on the doorknob and turned.

Francisco stood in front of her in all of his lean, buff, dimpled glory and gave her his slightly accented greeting, "Hello."

Pulling the door fully open, Natalia moved out of his way so he could walk in, then locked it securely behind him.

"Are you watching a scary movie in here?" Francisco asked with a mischevious smile. "I thought I heard a scream."

"No." Natalia crossed her arms and pouted a bit. "I was just startled, that's all. You're late."

"Yes. I know. I am so sorry. One of your older neighbors had so many bags of groceries I decided to ride with her to help her out."

Ugh. Natalia rolled her eyes, unsure if he was the perfect man or a perfectly trained liar and manipulator.

Francisco placed a brown paper bag on the counter and walked over to where Natalia stood. He leaned over and gently kissed each of her cheeks in greeting. She inhaled at the curve of his neck when he leaned close to reach her, and along with a hint of his alluring cologne, she inhaled a powerful wiff of electrical fire. As he pulled away, he met her eyes only inches from hers and smiled just enough to drive her mad.

Taking advantage of his closeness, Natalia spun him forty-five degrees and pressed his back against the wall. His coy smile returned with amusement, and he leaned down to gently press his lips to hers. *Whew. Not gay,* Natalia thought, relieved. He was sexy but so gentle and sweet when all Natalia wanted to do was rip his clothes off then and there. She knew how he felt about her. She could smell it in the air. If she didn't know better, she would've thought every appliance in the kitchen had caught fire. But, to erase all potential doubt from his mind, she reached behind her, unzipped her dress, and let it fall to the ground.

His gentle approach turned more passionate and animalistic as he spun around and pinned her against the wall. He kissed her neck while his hands explored her nearly naked body when a bang at the door made them both scream.

Daniel opened the door kicking a package in from the hallway. He looked shocked and embarrassed to see what he had walked in on.

"Oh, gosh. I'm sorry. I..." Daniel said, stumbling over his words, his eyes averted to the ground.

Natalia pushed Francisco away and ran to the countertop in the kitchen, grabbed the paper bag, and ran it into her room.

She returned less than a minute later to find the two men staring at each other. She stepped between them, two fully dressed men and her, standing in her bra and panties.

There didn't seem to be anything to say, so she just let it go, walked over to Francisco, grabbed her dress, and pulled it back on.

"So, I'm Daniel," her brother said, trying to break the silence. "I'm Natalia's half-bra... oh gosh, I mean half-bro, ugh, brother. Geez."

"Daniel, this is Francisco. Can we have a minute?"

"Oh, yeah. Sorry. What was I thinking, just standing here? Ahhh." Daniel said, crossing his eyes like he was crazy. "So, nice to meet you, Fernando."

"Francisco," Natalia corrected.

Daniel walked down the hallway to his room, uncomfortably muttering something to himself.

"So, Fernando," Natalia began seductively, dragging a finger down his chest. "Is what I need in that bag?"

"Yes," he replied, not at all frazzled. "Blow it in someone's face, put it in their drink, bake it in their food, whatever. You don't need much, but you have to be sure you do not inhale it yourself or get it on your skin. Be very careful with it."

"Aw, thanks," Natalia said, opening the door for Francisco to leave.

"Let me know when you need another delivery," he said with a smile.

Ugh, the dimples.

"I'll text you my next order," Natalia said as she closed the door and walked over to her phone by the couch.

A new message arrived from Bunny containing the contact information for Mr. George Hathaway. Natalia saved the contact, then, with a girlish giggle, sent Francisco an eggplant emoji.

Damn Buffets

Buffets had always disgusted Natalia. The popular selections were rotated out regularly with fresh replacements, but other items on the buffet line sat for hours. The hot meals crusted over due to the heat radiating from the warm water underneath. The cold items became gelatinous or wilted. People with varying levels of hygiene hovered over the same food, with body hairs, dandruff, and boogers sneaking under the edge of the sneeze guard. Plus, everyone has seen that person who grabs a piece of chicken with their hand because the tongs are on the other side or scratch their nuts before fondling the salad dressing scoop.

However, Natalia was sure of the specific instance that inspired her anti-buffet lifestyle.

***

She recalled the one time her mother took her out to eat as a child. She was unsure if it was always going to be a one-time thing or, because of the experience, it became a one-time thing. They walked into the restaurant, hand in hand, then up to the register to purchase two buffet plates and two drinks. As they walked to their seats, Natalia glanced through the door to the kitchen to see a woman holding a garden hose over the iced tea dispenser, filling it with water.

The hose was likely used to transport the water from the sink, but the idea of a garden hose filling the container made her stomach turn. She sat down at the table while her mother filled their drinks.

When Natalia saw Tatiana return to the table with two sweet teas, her stomach rumbled in disgust.

"What's the problem, my little, odd bird? I thought you would enjoy going out to eat."

"Nothing. I'm just hungry, I guess," she replied.

They picked up their plates and walked over to the buffet. Natalia began to fill her plate with items from the hot bar. These foods that would never go together in a standard restaurant: like fried chicken, egg rolls, pizza, spaghetti, and pigs in a blanket.

"Natalia, don't you think you should have a salad instead?" her mom asked with an air of superiority from the cold section of the buffet.

Natalia looked down at her now full plate and wondered what to do with the food she had if she wanted to get a salad. Should she put the food back? She hadn't touched anything with her hands, but they did touch her plate. Deciding against dumping her already selected food, she walked over to the salad bar and placed a layer of lettuce atop her other food to appease her mother.

They sat down and placed their paper napkins on their laps. Natalia's mother took dainty bites of her salad, careful not to take too much and have a full mouth or drop any food on herself. Natalia looked around at the other tables. One would think the display of desperate, over- consumption would be enough to make her turn away, but she couldn't take her eyes off these people who were stuffing themselves just so they could return to the trough and slop more on their plates. The scene looked less like dining than a competition, a competition to see if you could beat the restaurant and eat more food than you paid for.

"Hey. Weirdo." Tatiana snapped her fingers in front of Natalia's face to break her trance. "Stop staring."

"Sorry," she said as she looked down, embarrassed.

Tatiana always called her nasty names. She expected it, but it still hurt her feelings. Natalia picked up her fork and poked at a soggy piece of lettuce until she could get it to stay on her fork. Just as she was bringing it up to her mouth, she saw what would scar her for the rest of her life. A large, sweaty man wearing an oversized V-neck t-shirt that looked thinner than one-ply toilet paper, grass-stained, grey sweatpants, and stretched-out suspenders that were not quite doing their job, allowing his jolly belly to hang over his pants and the very upper crease of his butt crack showing through his near transparent shirt. His appearance, however, was oddly not the problem. The man was standing at the dessert bar with two full plates. Cakes, brownies, and pies were piled high on each plate and drowned in whipped cream. But, as he was walking to his seat, she saw the man take notice of the glorious chocolate fountain. She watched him, her fork frozen inches from her mouth, as he was obviously debating how to use the chocolate fountain with both of his hands full. He looked back and forth between his plates and the fountain, sometimes moving a plate toward the slowly dripping chocolate before pulling it back.

Natalia finally forked the lettuce into her mouth and chewed slowly, still watching how this man would solve his dilemma. She watched as he checked both ways over his shoulder to see if anyone was around, and to her surprise, he bent over and opened his mouth, allowing the chocolate to run directly over his lips. Some of the chocolate made it into his mouth, but the bulk of it rolled off his face and lips and back into the circulating fountain.

Natalia gasped, choking on her lettuce. She coughed and heaved, trying to dislodge the greens, when her mother pushed her sweet tea closer.

"Take a drink," she whispered sternly. "You are embarrassing me. Everyone is looking at us."

Natalia continued coughing and pushed the drink away, catching a crack in the table and sending hose-water iced tea all over her mother's lap.

Tatiana jumped out of her seat, sending perfect little ice cubes falling to the floor, except for the few wedged in her cleavage. She grabbed Natalia by the hand and ran the two of them out as fast as she could.

***

Standing in the lobby of George Hathaway's, favorite buffet, she realized she *was* likely the reason her mom never took her out again. And to think that what normally bothered Tatiana about Natalia, her odd sense of smell, had nothing to do with what went down. The scene was almost entirely caused by her totally normal sense of sight.

Natalia was dressed in a white button-down shirt and khaki pants. She could pass as a customer, but most people would assume she worked there. It was probably like wearing a red polo shirt to Target. After taking in her surroundings, Natalia walked with confidence and purpose to the kitchen. No one paid her any mind. Even a manager walked by and didn't give her a second glance. She walked to the back and saw a dozen drink carafes lined up against the wall by the sink. Not all looked like they were intended for sweet tea, George's favorite. A few looked like they might just be for water, and another couple for some type of lemonade. When she reached the end of the line, she was surprised, yet not at all surprised, that a short four-foot hose was filling them. Natalia sighed at the predictability of hourly workers and nonchalantly walked back past the sink, dropping the ricin powder she acquired from Francisco's connection into each container, careful not to get any on her skin or to even breathe until she was out of the kitchen.

George was a sucker for sweet tea, which was why he frequented this particular buffet. Not many restaurants served sweet tea north of Virginia, and Natalia knew that sweetening your own tea wasn't the same. From watching him during his last few visits to the establishment, he filled up his plate and cup at least half a dozen times. Despite the signs posted all around the restaurant, on tables, and on each buffet table, George was notorious for reusing his same plate with each refill. If there was ever a line, he cut in front of people. He probably knew his days were numbered and didn't have the time to wait. Not only was his behavior rude and disgusting, but his blatant disregard for the rules had her eager to end his life.

The waitstaff and management talked to George about his behavior numerous times, but rather than lose their best customer, they now turned a blind eye. Although he seemed to enjoy using the same plate over and over, he only used a napkin once. Dab a blob of ketchup off his lip, then crumble it up and toss it aside. Got a little ranch on his chin? Wipe it off, crumble the napkin, and toss. When he was finally finished with his meal, his table contained one plate and a pile of napkins, many of which would have fallen to the floor. At one time, the bus boys would pick up his napkins between his trips to the buffet, but after much complaining about the mess he left, his non-tipping, and his disgusting presence, the manager finally agreed that no one had to talk to or clean up after the slob until he left.

After following her assigned retiree week in and week out, she concluded that most people who live to enjoy retirement are healthy and at least somewhat fit. George, however, was an exception to that rule. He looked like a walking heart attack—seeing that he always skipped the salad bar and went straight for the fried foods, there was no question why. Plus, drinking five or six tall glasses of sweet tea each meal, his blood sugar levels had to be off the charts. How did an artery-clogged diabetic live this long?

A few months ago, Natalia would have been more cautious about distributing a bio-toxin-like ricin in a public area. But she was over caring. People would get sick, some would die, and hopefully, one of them would be George.

***

After stopping in the bathroom to wash her hands and change her shirt, Natalia secretly wished she could stay. She didn't want to watch George gluttonously stuff himself, following each large bite with an audible slurp of sweet tea. Neither did she actually want to watch him die. He was gross enough in life. What Natalia really wanted to stay and watch was the reactions on the faces of the disgusted patrons forced to eat anywhere near the pig, or even the staff who had been cleaning up after the slob week after week. Not many people celebrated death, but she had sneaking suspicion that none of these people would grieve.

The clanging of plates, glasses and silverware filled the room over the hum of conversation in the background. With the fear of accidentally poisoning herself growing in her gut, Natalia couldn't get out of the restaurant quick enough, but with each step the sounds grew louder and the distance between her and the door grew longer like a hallway stretching out narrowly in front of her.

Had she poisoned herself after all? It wasn't as if she wore protective gear like a face mask or hazmat suit; nothing subtle about that. Natalia had been careful though. Francisco was concerned about her using the deadly substance, but refused to ask questions. He simply explained the need for extreme caution and let it go. When she finally reached the lobby, her legs were heavy, like she was walking in wet concrete.

A voice echoed from her right as she passed a dad walking hand in hand with his son, "Can I have some tea, daddy?"

"Just this once, son. It's a birthday treat," the dad replied.

Natalia nearly threw up, but shoved through the double glass doors just in time to take a deep breath of fresh air. She continued walking to the curb where she sad and placed her head between her knees and wondered if she had gone too far.

DANIEL IN THE LIONS' DEN

Stuart and Bunny invited Daniel and Natalia over for drinks on a Friday evening.

As far as Daniel knew, he worked for Stuart, and Natalia worked for Bunny, but as Natalia followed him off the penthouse elevator and watched him make his way over to the couple, greeting him from the other side of the room, she couldn't help but compare him to Daniel in the Lions' Den. She had really bonded with Stuart and Bunny, even more so than with Daniel. But she realized that was because she still put on an act for him. The three of them were nothing like him. He had no idea who they were. He had no idea what they were capable of. He was blameless and ignorant of the schemes the others cooked up, and she knew there was a chance, if she was not more careful, that her naive brother would be the one to pay the price, one way or another.

***

Stuart and Bunny met Daniel halfway, exchanging pleasantries, hand-shakes, and hugs before working their way over to Natalia. One nervous look at Stuart, and he knew she was anxious about the four of them being together, having not discussed how to hide their working relationship.

Stuart threw an arm around her shoulder, kissed her on the cheek, and spoke quietly into her ear, "You do you, my dear."

He gently grabbed her hand and placed it at his bent elbow as if escorting her into the room, only pausing momentarily so she and Bunny could exchange kisses on the cheek. Natalia thought she caught a glimpse of temporary disgust or maybe even a tinge of jealousy in Daniel's expression, but it quickly passed. It must be hard for other men to feel worthy around someone like Stuart, who so effortlessly commanded a room.

As Stuart and Bunny's chef, Maria placed dozens of dishes filled with amazing-looking food along the dining room table, Bunny spoke up.

"You two are in luck. Maria has made her famous Tapas for us this evening, she said, pointing with her arm in a spokesmodel arm motion over the spread.

The table was made of old driftwood, not quite evened out along the sides but very long and narrow. Natalia wondered if when people sat across from each other at the table if their knees touched. She may never know, as tonight was a fill-your-plate-and-take-a-seat kind of dinner.

"Looks delicious," Daniel piped up. "I hear buffets are all the rage." He winked and chuckled under his breath.

Natalia was quite sure the others knew what he was referring to, but not only was it not funny and way too soon to joke about a tragic event, but no one really knew how to react, except Maria, of course, who was proud expression turned angry and embarrassed as she had never heard anyone refer to her exquisite tapas as a buffet.

"You know," Daniel said, trying to explain and walk back the insult he didn't realize he had made. "All those people got sick and died at that buffet this week in the suburbs. I mean, it really looks amazing, Maria. Thank you for treating us to a piece of your homeland."

Maria rolled her eyes and left the room in a huff.

"She's from Jersey, Daniel," Stuart said, slightly amused as if he was almost enjoying Daniel's awkwardness, even if it was at the expense of his employee. "You sure rubbed her the wrong way."

"That was something, though, wasn't it?" Stuart continued. "It will be a cold night in Hell before that restaurant opens up again."

"The restaurant closed?" Natalia looked up at Stuart. She had been avoiding the news not wanting to hear the final report on her collateral damage. Seeing it on the news made it real.

"Couldn't they just close up and clean everything?"

"When nearly two dozen people die of organ failure after food poisoning from a restaurant, you can pretty much assume they're going under." Stuart took a bite of a bacon-wrapped date and continued, "Authorities are saying it was some kind of domestic terrorism or maybe a disgruntled worker. They're certain it was poison and likely an isolated event, but no business is coming back from that. "

Stuart continued filling his plate, but Bunny placed her plate back down on the table as if she had lost her appetite. As Natalia watched her walk away, she inhaled an overpowering scent of old garbage.

The smell hit her like a slap to the face. It had been a while since she smelled the familiar stink of being second-guessed. Along with disappointment, it was the smell of her childhood, after all. Every time Natalia knew what her mother was thinking, every time she came home with a complaint from the teacher or fellow students about something weird she said, every time she brought up her bizarre sense of smell, every time she behaved in a way that embarrassed her mother in public... garbage, garbage, garbage, garbage. And it wasn't the smell of trash; it was garbage. It smelled of rotten meat, spoiled milk, and decayed vegetables; all left out in a hot, enclosed space for days.

Her mother always told her, "Wipe that disgusted look off your face." Natalia wouldn't dare explain that her nose crinkled and her nostrils flared because of her mom's smell.

But Natalia was used to her bitter, sour, rotten mom smelling of garbage. What she couldn't get used to was her beautiful and kind friend taking on that scent.

Stuart didn't seem at all bothered by the additional and unnecessary deaths... it was the cost of doing business, but it was now more apparent than ever that Bunny was. Maybe Natalia was getting a bit sloppy. Just because it was easier to add something to all of the drinks doesn't mean that was the right way to go about it. In her mind, and probably Stuart's, the crime was even less obvious when a her mark died with others in a large group. Then it is clearly not a hit job, right?

But Natalia *did* care what Bunny thought and would try to be more cautious not to hurt innocent bystanders along the way. She walked over to the expansive windows where Bunny had drifted after leaving her plate behind. Natalia stood right next to her, hearing but not listening to the conversation the men were having back at the table.

"I can tell you're upset. I'll do better."

Bunny forced a smile that didn't quite reach her eyes. Lavender. She knew Bunny didn't like it but knew it was part of the situation they were in now. She placed her arm around Natalia's waist, gave her a slight squeeze, and they walked back to the table to rejoin the men eyeing the neon *You Do You* sign on the wall. The tacky sign looked more out of place than ever.

THOSE ARE NOT CHOCOLATE CANDIES

Walter was very much like the stereotypical dad Natalia had always imagined most normal kids had growing up. Being a Millennial, she still had a very fifties ideology for families. This is what happens when most of your understanding of life comes from internet videos. Full episodes of old sitcoms are posted for the world to see.

Walter's kids were now grown, but he lived a short block away from his youngest son, who had two young children of his own. He was very active in his grandchildren's lives, which seemed to be his inspiration for keeping in good shape. He routinely took long walks through the neighborhood, followed by old-school calisthenics in his driveway.

After two weeks of watching Walter, Natalia was unsure she could go through with *removing him* from the pension plan, so to speak. He was a widower who visited his wife's grave daily, an active and helpful grandparent, a neighbor who always chipped in, and he made weekend meal deliveries for the soup kitchen. Maybe her doubts also had a little to do with Bunny's influence on her.

Walter had a standing appointment with his grandchildren to go to a Kids Hour show at the local movie theater. Kids Hour was a weekly showing of a children's television show on the big screen, at a moderate volume, with the lights only partially dimmed. She had followed him into the theater earlier this week, but after only five minutes of listening to a bald four-year-old's annoying voice, she was afraid if she didn't leave, she would murder everyone in the theater. On her way out, however, she overheard him telling his grandkids he would be back at the theater to watch a special screening of one of his favorite movies with his "old cronies" later in the week.

He tried to explain the plot line to the kids, but they took more interest in the sound of their sneakers on the sticky floor.

Natalia decided to get tickets to the throwback screening for Friday night, but when she was on the theater's website to buy her ticket, Daniel called from work.

"Hey, Daniel."

"Hi. What are you doing?" he asked.

Unprepared to offer a believable alibi, she simply said, "I'm online ordering tickets to see a special screening of some old movie this Friday."

Natalia hadn't heard of the movie before, so she started to read the description over the phone.

"No way! Of course, I know it! I love that movie. It was one of my dad's favorites." He paused. "Our dad, I mean."

She didn't know this, but she knew so little about the man; why would she know his favorite movie?

"Who are you going with? Oh, let me guess, that Fredrico guy, right? I don't know about him, Natalia. Did you say he works in a spa? Don't you want someone who can better support you?" Daniel asked.

She hadn't planned to bring Francisco to a killing, but she almost wanted to now. *What the hell was Daniel talking about? Whatever gave him the idea that she needed support. What was his big problem with Francisco, and why the hell could he never remember his name?* She could've easily made up a name, said she was going on a date with someone else simply to appease him, or even thrown out Bunny's name instead, but she, again, decided to just come out with the truth.

"I was planning to go alone. Do you want to go? I can get your ticket while I am ordering mine."

She stood up and paced around the room, wondering what the hell she was doing...she had worked so hard to keep this other side of her a secret, yet she had just invited Daniel to a movie where she planned to, most likely, kill someone. Although she still had not found anything about Walter worth killing for. Maybe she never would, and this Friday would end up just being a nice night out with her big brother. If it didn't work out, she would ping Bunny for a new contact.

Realizing Daniel was still talking on the other end of the phone, she thought it was probably important to listen. However, she soon realized he was just singing his favorite songs from the movie, almost making her hang up the phone.

***

She despised musicals. She always had. During her childhood, her tone-deaf mother sang show tunes all day long.

Natalia would ask her, "How can you stand all that singing? Don't you find it distracting?"

"You odd little bird. Everyone loves musicals. The songs are all part of the story."

"But, isn't it odd that two people will just be going about their business having a drink, riding the train, or walking through the park, and then, out of nowhere, one of them will just break out in song?"

"Oh, Natalia. You're such a weirdo. Most people just accept it for what it is in all of its beauty and do not try to read into it so much. What's wrong with you? How did I raise someone so uncultured?"

***

Daniel's melody finally ended, so she could hang up without showing her true feelings to him. After all, how would she explain to him why someone who despises musicals would be going to see one alone?

***

Friday evening came and Natalia and Daniel arrived at the theater just as the doors opened. They grabbed a bag of red licorice, a box of chocolate-covered raisins, and two bottles of water, then took a seat in the middle of the last row. The room was dim but not dark, with directional lighting along the stairs and low-level classical music playing in the background. The theater started to fill, and Natalia feared she would not be close enough to Walter to keep an eye on him, let alone do any harm. But just as she doubted her initial plan of arriving first, Walter walked in with another man. The two men may have been the same age, but Walter's friend was more frail with less hair. His skin was like stretched-out leather that looked soft and two sizes too big. He looked like someone who lost an extreme amount of weight long after the elasticity in his skin was gone. Without the saggy skin, he would likely look younger, and she surmised that years of being overweight was hell on his joints, hence the fragile look when he walked.

As luck would have it, the two men sat directly in front of them. Usually, this would bother her. Isn't it always the tall man who sits in front of short women in theaters? But in this case, she was pleased to have him so close. She also appreciated that there were no cup holders in this theater, so Walter and his friend placed their drinks on the floor between sips.

She felt the pressure of the choke wire in her right jeans pocket and was thankful the pants were a size too big, so the outline was not visible. In her left pocket, she had two small bottles of eye drops. She hoped not to have to poison this guy, but she needed a backup plan if an opportunity to choke him didn't present itself.

Daniel muttered something beside her about a rock in his shoe, but her attention was on where Walter placed his drink on the floor. It was a bit of a reach for her, especially with Daniel watching, but she could make it work if necessary.

At the strong smell of sharp vinegar and cheese, her attention was quickly brought back to Daniel and his shoe. She noticed that not only did he get the rock out, but he, for some unknown reason, decided to take his shoes off. She looked at him with her eyes wide and mouth open in amazement, about to tell him to put his stank-ass shoes back on when the lights dimmed, and the speakers blared the previews.

Her nostrils flared in disgust as she battled through the beginning of the movie, trying to keep her emotions in check. She tried to take her mind off the smell and the annoying singing, but unfortunately for her, Daniel decided it was appropriate to sing along. Then he laughed loud enough for an elderly couple sitting several rows up to turn around. He was oblivious to their stares and seemed to be truly enjoying himself. He was sitting on the edge of his seat with a child-like grin in anticipation of what he knew, by heart, was next.

Natalia clenched her fists, trying not to lose her cool. She watched the cheesy, musical interaction of the cast and decided to excuse herself.

"I need to use the bathroom," she whispered to Daniel.

His eyes didn't leave the screen, and she was unsure if he even heard her. On the plus side, she was no longer concerned with him watching her too closely.

She scooted past several people on the end of the row, walked down the theater stairs in the near dark, and out into the brightly lit hallway. Not knowing where to go, since she really didn't have to pee, she walked all the way to the other end of the building, slowly passing the men's room.

Being a woman meant a lifetime of long bathroom lines in public places. Planning to murder someone in a men's bathroom, however, seemed less of a hassle. As she expected, there were no men waiting in line. She eyed the doorway all the way down the hall to see if anyone went in or out, and no one did.

Natalia made her way back to her seat, past the angry knees of the people that she had to walk in front of. Daniel looked as though he hadn't moved a muscle, like a kid in the eighties sitting on the floor in front of the family television on a Saturday morning. His frozen smile was still in place, his ass still on the edge of his chair and his mouth slightly agape, causing her to wonder if drool would soon fall to the already sticky floor. She was pretty sure he didn't even see her sit back down.

"The line was too long," she whispered, leaning back, giving herself another reason to get up and leave if her mark gave her the opportunity.

Taking time out to watch Walter, Natalia only saw a sweet, considerate man sitting quietly with his hands on his lap, occasionally taking a silent sip from his drink and quietly placing it back down.

Natalia bit her lip and looked back and forth between sweet Walter and his very large soda. Surely he would have to use the bathroom soon... or was it a sign that maybe she should leave Walter untouched.

Suddenly, the wet sound of chewy candy and saliva being sloshed around made its way to Natalia's ears. She closed her eyes and, under her breath, said, "You've got to be kidding me."

Daniel ignored her, not rendering her annoyance in the slightest. He went on to pour more chocolates into his mouth, but this time, neglecting to close it. Natalia stared at him, debating on whether to say something or not, but he probably couldn't even hear her while he was chewing that loud. More trying to escape the sound than anything, Natalia bent down to reach for her drink. She took a small sip and then stretched to place the drink as close to Walter's drink as she could. It was a stretch, but it could be done. At least now her drink was near his to give her an excuse for reaching down there. She only needed to wait until happy singing returned.

It wasn't long before another random character belted out a song mid-conversation, and again, Daniel joined in. It wouldn't surprise her if, at this point, Walter turned around and stabbed him, but, of course, he continued to be the perfect gentleman.

Natalia leaned back further and further as if trying to escape the singing with the accompanying sound effects of raisin sticking to his teeth. Walter's buddy reached over to offer him candy. Walter held out his hand as his stingy friend poured two measly blobs into his hand. As irritated as Natalia was, Walter was nothing, if not the thankful picture of grace. At this point in the night, Natalia was more inclined to kill her brother than Walter. Daniel's off-key singing and open-mouthed chewing, combined with his stinky feet, would've been reason enough for her to pass a death sentence on someone else. But her brother was the only family she had.

Without warning, Walter jumped up so quickly that the surrounding rows looked over in shock. Natalia had assumed he wouldn't be getting up to use the bathroom or get more snacks, but she straightened herself in her chair to follow him out. She glanced down the row to see how deep into the movie the people were that she would have to walk by again, but their eyes were not on the movie. They were on Walter, who had not moved from the spot where he initially and abruptly stood.

"Someone help! He's choking!" Walter's friend screamed, trying to angle himself to wrap his arms around Walter's ribs. The frail man was a bit shorter than Walter, and he couldn't get his arms in the right position.

Daniel stood up and attempted to step over the row of seats to help, but having removed his shoes earlier, his slippery socked feet slipped through the crack between the seat back and the seat, wedging him in place with his other leg still in the back row.

Chaos ensued while at least a dozen people could be heard calling emergency services while women in formal dresses sang and danced on the big screen in the background. As time passed and more people attempted to get to Walter, he began to frantically throw himself onto the seat backs of the row in front of him as if trying to Heimlich himself.

The theater lights came on and Natalia was granted an up close and personal view of death. Walter was on his back in front of the seats which were all tilted up, giving her more visibility. Walter's eyes were open, so much so that it looked like his eyelids fell behind the eyeballs themselves. They seemed to be one push away from popping out of the sockets. His kind eyes that had onced looked upon his doting grandchildren were bright red and drops of blood puddled like tears in the corners. Blood vessels formed patterned webbing over his face that could only barely be detected in his blue skin.

Daniel pulled on her sleeve as ushers directed everyone out of the theater.

When Natalia and Daniel made their way out to the parking lot, she was tempted to ask him if she could run back inside and use the bathroom, but when two large firetrucks and an ambulance pulled up, she decided it was better to just leave.

"Did you see the chocolate on the back of that man's pants?" Daniel asked, more to himself than anything.

His shoulders were slumped over, and his hands were shoved deep into his pockets. Natalia couldn't tell if he was teasing or if he was upset by the tragedy that unfolded, literally, in front of him.

"I don't think that was chocolate, Daniel," Natalia said with a small chuckle.

She didn't know if he heard her or not as he kicked rubble on the sidewalk with his feet, keeping his eyes on the ground. She was amazed that someone could get torn up over someone they didn't know. Sure, Walter seemed like a great guy, and she wasn't even sure if she could have gone through with killing him, but Daniel didn't know that.

Trying to fight her aggravation, she put on her compassionate mask and asked, "Are you okay?"

Daniel kicked something else on the sidewalk that looked more like litter than sidewalk rubble, only pulling his hand out of his pocket to pick a raisin out of his teeth when she received a more disappointing answer than she expected.

"I can't believe they didn't offer us a refund."

***

Natalia's eyes were fixed on her bathroom mirror. Staring at her reflection as a child was a luxury, but as she stared deep into her own green eyes, she knew it was time for some self evaluation. She blamed her mother for making her an outcast. Years of being locked in your home will make even the most social butterfly awkward and out of place. But did her mother lock her away because she was different, or did the emotional torment make her so? It was your typical *which-came-first argument, the chicken or the egg*.

It was a big weekend for Natalia. After Walter choked to death at the theater, she eliminated three more contacts in the tri-state area. An apparent suicide in the Bronx, a burglary gone wrong in Hoboken, and the body of an old man with a phallic-sounding name dumped in the Hudson River. She was good at her job. Should she be proud of herself?

As she continued to allow herself to inspect every aspect of her reflection, she heard Daniel in the other room. She eyed the goosebumps as they appeared on her forearms. Why did she suddenly feel she was in the company of a stranger?

She was taken aback by Daniel's reaction when Walter collapsed during the movie. He was callous and indifferent, having witnessed something that most people would view as traumatic. Not Natalia, but most normal people. Yet, Daniel had been so visibly shaken with disappointment that he was unable to watch the end of the film or get a refund. He hadn't even bought the tickets. Sure, Daniel was socially awkward in a way that made other people embarrassed for him, but she had never witnessed the emotional detachment before. Perhaps Natalia's *crazy gene* wasn't from her mother but from their shared father. For the first time, she saw a distorted glimmer of herself in Daniel's coldness. Turns out, they were family.

working for on the weekend

Daniel was the only one in the office on Saturday morning. His first month with the company was focused on learning the ins and outs of MBI. He studied the company's policies and procedures and came to understand key personnel. He vigilantly worked to evaluate and strengthen the Corporate Risk Management plan, one of Stuart's top priorities for Daniel's first month. Although Daniel specialized in this field and had bolstered the insurance plans covering key corporate assets, that wasn't why he was working over the weekend. He also wanted to review the actuals from his first thirty days as CFO. Analyzing the numbers and trends excited Daniel and got him out of bed in the morning.

Daniel was determined to outwork everyone. He never wanted to be out of work again. The long eight months of looking for a new job took its mental toll. Scaling down his way of living, his wardrobe, and his style had been at risk, not to mention that he was only days from being unable to make rent. Although he had been CFO at three start-ups before, this was M-fucking-BI, a formerly top-ranked company. MBI was big time. Daniel would not fail. He could not fail. This was more than a job to him. It was his career and future livelihood. He would put in whatever hours necessary to be successful.

Working Saturdays proved fruitful. Daniel's organizational skills, trending analysis, and expertise in tax laws had paid off. For the first time in years, MBI actually had a profitable month. Stuart had reported consistent break-even numbers since he took over as CEO, but this was the first month in the black... and it perfectly aligned with Daniel's starting the company.

Daniel's reporting and historical trending data showed the potential for a strong future. The only outlying data point was in the recurring payments for the pension program. The latest expense was lower than any in recent history. It made sense, he supposed, with the program being canceled and people getting old and dying. But a dozen retirees passed instead of the norm of one to two people a month. And in fact, a lot of the people who departed were high-salaried managerial and even executive types.

Daniel studied the charts and numbers and knew the pension payments were out of his control. He thought back to something Stuart told him about gray areas and only worrying about controlling what you could control... and influencing what you can't.

With so many life-changing events coinciding, from Natalia coming into his life, landing his dream job, and now pulling MBI into the black, he almost felt selfish, but he would happily take the win.

Having been at the office all day and the clock approaching 9 p.m., he was getting hungry, but he knew there was one more thing he had to take care of before he could leave. Stuart made it very clear that all corporate training courses had to be completed within forty-five days of hire. Daniel had diligently completed all but one—*Code of Conduct*.

After logging in and clicking through to the training, Daniel scanned slide after slide about company policies. *Intellectual property, dress code, blah, blah, blah.* There was even a section that covered the company's *Morality Clause.* Daniel assumed this was some kind of catch-all clause to protect the company image, allowing them to "fire with cause" for embarrassing situations like surfing porn at work, illicit public affairs, and posting anti-company propaganda online. When Daniel reached the section about inappropriate behavior, he chuckled. He had been told in the past that his comments and behaviors could be misconstrued and that he could make others feel awkward. But, according to the training, since he had never had an intra-office relationship and was careful not to touch coworkers... not even a pat on the back, he knew he was golden. Not to mention that his department was male-dominated, like most math-related careers.

It did bother him the way Stuart so blatantly kissed Natalia's hand when she came to the office, but she didn't work there after all. Daniel smirked to himself when he realized how quickly he fell into the role of the over-protective half-brother.

"Report complaints to your manager or the Human Resources department, blah, blah, blah."

Daniel quickly skipped through the remaining slides and signed off on his training. There would always be things that were out of his control. But he could control getting his training done on time and staying on top of his reports, even if it meant working on the weekend.

He almost didn't want to check into the anomalies with the pension fund, the numbers did make Daniel and the company look good after all.

Anytime, Brother

Stuart spent his morning leadership team conference call on a massage table while Brynhildr leaned her two-hundred-fifty-pound frame into a knot he had in between his shoulder blades. Stuart congratulated the team, specifically Daniel, on the company's first profitable month in years. As he lay with his face in the massage table cradle, he could feel the tension through the speaker phone. The celebrations sounded genuine, but he could picture Daniel sitting awkwardly, unsure how to handle the praise and recognition. He normally didn't have any trouble handling stress or dealing with people uncomfortable with his ways, but he has been getting a different vibe lately from Daniel.

In a meeting later that day, Stuart walked into Daniel analyzing data from the pension fund. He was asking questions about the retired CFO and the estimates he came up with for the annual payments to the plan. He was reaching out to the other people on the executive team for help gathering information, turning over rocks Stuart wanted left unturned.

Inserting himself into Daniel's conversation, Stuart added, "I worked closely with Old Man Johnson when he developed the budget for the pension plan. I am happy to review the numbers with you. Plus, budgets are made to be revised." Stuart smiled at his team, receiving a warm reaction from everyone except Daniel. He cleared his throat and continued,

"That's why we re-forecast every month. Our strengths and weaknesses change, as do our priorities. We need to remain flexible and able to adapt in real-time."

Stuart had been speaking to the entire group but now looked directly at Daniel. "I can help you navigate the complexities of the pension process, especially since we just sunset the program before you arrived," Stuart offered before adding, "Change is the only constant, am I right?"

Daniel rigidly stacked his papers, tapped them on the table to straighten the pile, slid them into his folder, and sat down with his arms crossed like he was a spoiled toddler just sent to time out. Stuart tried to interpret his behavior but couldn't figure out why he would act like a child. It wasn't like Stuart had shut down his inquiry. He actually offered to help. For the rest of the meeting, Daniel wouldn't make eye contact with Stuart and only chimed in when called upon by someone else. When they wrapped up the meeting, he stormed out so quickly that Stuart couldn't even get a chance to check in with him or schedule a time to meet.

A few people stopped Stuart with random questions or kiss-ass comments on his way to catch up to Daniel. These interruptions slowed Stuart's pursuit, but he was able to catch a glimpse of his back as Daniel entered the staff lounge. Stuart approached the slightly ajar door to the breakroom and listened intently.

"So, as I was saying. I have some concerns about some blurred ethical lines." Stuart heard Daniel continue.

There must be another person in there with him, Stuart thought to himself.

"Look, man. I'm mid-level HR... I only handle administrative tasks like payroll and benefits. You need to see someone more senior about an ethical issue. That is way above my pay grade."

Stuart recognized the voice as Jackson Brahm.

Why did Daniel go to Jackson? Stuart wondered to himself.

Why go to HR unless it had to do with another employee?

Why this guy instead of Georgia O'Mally, the VP of Human Resources?

Did Daniel think Georgia would be loyal to Stuart, so he went down the ladder?

Stuart was beginning to worry that Daniel's financial analysis may be thorough enough for him to piece together Stuart's scheme to shrink the pension pool. On the one hand, Stuart was surprisingly proud of Daniel for all of his due diligence and for vetting the budget numbers. It was the type of work he needed in a CFO, but he certainly didn't expect from Daniel. But on the other hand, there was a lot at risk with Daniel digging too deep. Stuart needed to find out just how much Daniel knew.

"I don't want to put you in an uncomfortable position..." Daniel continued.

"Keep in mind that we are spread pretty thin right now. The layoffs hit the HR department, too, you know. Do you want me to hook you up with an HR manager to schedule a meeting?"

"You know, maybe this is a concern for the legal department," Daniel continued.

"What? Legal? What in the world would they have to do with this?" Jackson said, trailing off at the end as if he figured out a potential problem.

"Don't worry about it, brother."

Did Daniel just call Jackson "brother"? A black guy, and in the HR department, to boot?

"I'm talking about two separate things now. They are kind of the same in my mind, but really, it's two things, so just forget it. Thanks, man."

"Yeah, anytime, *brother*," Jackson said with a sharp sarcasm in his voice, particularly on the last word.

Stuart heard the quick clicks of shoes on the tile floor and knew Jackson was coming. Stuart looked down at his phone and leaned a shoulder against the wall. Jackson didn't even see Stuart as he turned in the other direction.

Daniel rounded the corner on Jackson's heels but turned right toward Stuart running into him.

"Woah, Danny Boy," Stuart said, throwing his arm over Daniel's shoulder. "Just the man I was looking for. You took off from the meeting so quickly that I didn't get to discuss your concerns. I should've known you would come here to the peon employee lounge. They always have better snacks in their vending machines, don't you think?"

Daniel laughed uncomfortably. "Yeah, I had to pee."

"Okay, TMI, Daniel. Just because we met in a bathroom doesn't mean I need to hear about all of your bathroom happenings."

"I mean, I left quickly because I needed to use the bathroom, then I just stopped here looking for someone."

"Is it a lady, Danny Boy? You know you need to be careful dating inside the company, right? Oh, is that why you were talking to Jackson?"

Daniel looked as if he had been caught with his hand in the cookie jar. "How did you..."

"I know things," Stuart said with a straight face. After a few seconds of watching Daniel squirm, he smiled and said, "He literally walked out right before you did."

"Oh, yeah. Jackson is a nice guy. We were just shooting the shit, you know, talking about the game last night," he replied.

"Really? What game?" Stuart asked.

"Doesn't matter," Daniel snapped quickly. "Anyway, I think I have what I need. I will call you to schedule a meeting if I have further budget questions. This is small-time stuff, way below your pay grade."

Stuart cringed. Not only had he just repeated a similar phrase to what Jackson used moments ago, but he was lying every step of the way. *What was he hiding? What did he know?*

Stuart removed his arm from Daniel's shoulder, patted him once on the back, and said, "Okay, man. I trust you. You're my guy."

Stuart turned and made his way back to his office, wishing he could find an excuse to ask security to pull up the video feed of Daniel's expression as he walked away.

SUSPICIOUS MINDS

It was a gloomy and overcast morning. The sun seemed to be taking a day off behind the clouds, buildings, or both. The window panes were sprinkled with raindrops that rolled down like sad tears into a puddle on the window frame. Daniel lay in his bed and stared at the patterns reflecting upon his ceiling, thinking about the whirlwind that his life had become. These last several months felt like a whole new chapter. His mother had been a big part of his life. She had always done everything for him. Even when he moved out, she paid his rent and bills, laundered his clothes, and prepared meals. He liked to joke that she was the perfect wife, which most people winced at for some reason. Since she had been gone, everything changed. He thought of her every day and missed her, but when he was being honest with himself, he could admit that it was what she did for him that he really missed. He didn't miss her nagging about finding a nice woman to settle down with, then turning around and criticizing any woman he brought home. He wouldn't miss the way she folded his underwear like origami. That was even too much for him. But losing her was like jumping into adulthood in one fell swoop. He had to learn to do so many tasks on his own for the first time. He initially comforted himself with thoughts of hiring a housekeeper, a cook, someone to pick up his laundry, etc. But, when he heard the surprising news of being cut out of her will on top of reaching the end of his latest severance pay that same week, he coped as best he could. He could finally accept that he missed what she did for him, but he really quite hated who she was.

Then, like an angel from heaven, Natalia came into his life. She was kind and sweet, though admittedly a bit quirky. She was an excellent cook, she liked to do the food shopping, she was happy to launder all of their clothes, and she kept their condo relatively clean. She filled the hole in his heart and fit herself into his life serendipitously. He often dreamed that Natalia was his mom, reincarnated, but his mom wasn't really ever as good of a person as Natalia initially seemed.

Daniel started to sweat and kicked off his blankets. He pushed the button on his bedside table to turn on the ceiling fan, then threw the remote across the room. He sighed, dropped his head back to the pillow, and tried to think about when things began to change. Like in every relationship, romantic or otherwise, the person you originally saw as amazing, brilliant, and flawless begins to show their true colors. Through the cracks in the veneer, Daniel began to see Natalia's annoying habits show through. Her once-perceived perfection melted into normalcy, and worst of all, he suspected his sweet half-sister of being darker and more manipulative than he had ever imagined.

It took a while for him to see what was right in front of his face. It all started as a suspicion when they would watch the news and one of those stories came on that made most moral, ethical human beings begin to doubt humanity, like a horrible murder, an adulterous relationship, or other unspeakable acts, he would sit horrified, she sat utterly unfazed or in some cases found it funny.

It was strange when he walked in on her entertaining Francisco that rather than hiding her state of undress, she jumped up and ran out of the room. He wondered what it was that she was hiding from him. Surely it wasn't her modesty since she seemed to feel perfectly comfortable running across the living room in her bra and panties rather than picking up the blanket where she was standing to cover herself.

Daniel pulled the sheet back over himself and rolled over, thinking of the moment that made him start to lock his bedroom door at night. The movie. Not the movie itself, obviously; that was a work of pure genius, but that whole night out with Natalia. He remembered being giddy at the movie, thrilled to find someone else who loved classic musicals. But, when the movie started, she didn't look excited or even the slightest bit interested. She just looked annoyed and anxious to get the movie over with. He was amazed that she left to use the bathroom, surely as any true fan would know, right before a big number. She didn't even bat an eye when she returned to her seat, walking right in front of people during a key scene. But, even with all of his attention on the movie itself, he still watched as she picked up her drink and slid it closer and closer to the man's drink in front of her. He couldn't get over the fact she seemed to intentionally go out of her way to place it right next to him, as inconvenient as it was to her. And with every stretch, he would catch a glimpse of a very expensive-looking watch on her arm that reminded him very much of Stuart's watch. Her behavior, her style, and her speech was becoming so oddly similar to his boss's that it disturbed him. Something was off with Natalia.

But, when the man in front of them jumped up choking, he knew. It was true that not everyone was panicking. Some people rushed to help. Others rushed to call an ambulance. While a few others sat frozen in place and stared in horror. But not Natalia. She sat in her seat, watching the man choke to death, more entertained than she had been for the entire movie. She sat back, reclined in her seat, tossing chocolates in her mouth. Her previously clenched fists and the annoyed look became somewhat relaxed. She looked happy, not content like she just ate a big meal but happy like she won the lottery. She completely lacked empathy or possibly even a moral compass.

Daniel was disappointed to miss the end of the movie, but more so was his disappointment in himself for painting his half-sister out to be something she clearly was not. Was it Natalia who pulled the wool over his eyes, or was it his need for someone to care for him that made her out to be exactly who he wanted? The girl who he thought was good may not be so after all. The half-sister he thought was kind was actually hateful. The woman that he thought was patient was impatient and irritable. The person he had invited into his home and life was not a blessing but a curse.

Drive Thru

Something was different about Daniel. He was more on edge, more skittish than usual. He was usually easy to read, but now, it was as if he was hiding a secret or nervous about something that he was afraid to talk about. He had asked Natalia if she wanted to go for a ride, which was the first strange sign since neither of them had a car.

"Do you mean on the subway? In a cab? On a tandem bike?" she joked.

"Uh, no," he said nervously. "I borrowed a car to run some errands in the suburbs.

Would you like to come with me? I thought we could spend the day together." His strained voice and his forced smile told Natalia that something else was up altogether, but being unsure of what it was, she agreed.

They drove in silence for close to an hour and were still only just outside of the city.

Natalia had her window rolled down and leaned her head out to feel the crisp breeze on her face. The air already felt fresher and cleaner, just being on the other side of the bridge. It made sense why dogs liked to ride with their heads out of the window. It felt amazing.

Daniel swerved around unidentifiable roadkill and scratched his head. She remembered this strange superstition from her dad. Whenever they would drive somewhere, which was not all that often, he would scratch his head at the sight of dead animals on the side of the road; he would say, "If you don't scratch your head when you see an animal carcass, you'll go bald."

She thought it was silly and never did it herself, but if she went bald one day, she'd know why.

"What the hell was that? It looked like a furry snake," Daniel whimpered, disgusted.

"It looked like a cat's tail," Natalia answered without missing a beat.

"A cat's tail? We just drove past flattened roadkill at sixty-five miles an hour, and you could identify it as a cat's tail? That's odd, Natalia. No offense, but that's really odd."

He called her odd.

He said it.

It actually happened.

She knew he was not *unique* like her, but she never thought he would call her names like her rotten bitch mom once did. If only he knew why she could identify the cat's tail. The word *odd* wouldn't come close to covering it. When she poisoned Miss. Jellybottom's cats, she kept the tails as souvenirs. It wasn't like a serial killer thing that psychological profilers talk about on crime shows or movies because she didn't do it for kicks. She poisoned the cats for research, cut off their tails, and hung them from the fence in the backyard in hopes of gaining some kind of attention from her mother. Any attention, even negative, was better than no attention at all.

Unfortunately, one dangling cat tail didn't do the trick. But neither did twenty dangling cat tails. Her mother either didn't care that assorted cat tails were hanging from their fence, or she didn't care that Natalia was crying out for her attention. Either way, she just didn't care, not about the tails, not about Natalia. All she cared about was that no one else knew how odd her daughter was, and she planned to keep it that way. In hindsight, perhaps hanging the tails on the front porch or the outside of the fence so that the neighbors could see would've done the trick. Reflecting back on the cat tails, she finally understood why Coach Cooley's usual tough-guy demeanor changed drastically when he walked through their backyard all those years ago. She'd always wondered why he ran.

Natalia leaned back on the headrest. She was comfortable in silence, thanks to years of being ignored as a child, but Daniel's constant fidgeting told her he felt otherwise. After clearing his throat several times as if preparing himself to say something, he finally verbalized his thoughts.

"I'm hungry." That was all he seemed to be able to manage.

"Hi, Hungry. I'm Natalia," she said with a laugh, hoping to get him to loosen up, but he didn't even smile.

"I think I'll pull over at a restaurant. Do you want anything?" Daniel asked, not taking his eyes off the road.

"No, thanks," she replied, resting her head against the door frame and taking in the significant number of trees.

Growing up, her mom normally fed her very healthy meals. She wasn't allowed to have sweets or fast food. She dreamed of being able to go out on her own and pick up some fatty or sugary food when she grew up. But there were times when Tatiana was feeling insecure that she would stuff Natalia like she was prepping her to be served up for dinner. Weeks would go by, and Natalia would catch Tatiana staring at her when she undressed, not at all in a sexual way, but in an admiring, jealous sort of way. Sitting near each other, she noticed Tatiana staring closely at her flawless, wrinkle-free skin. The more Tatiana admired what Natalia had, the more she recognized what she didn't. In the following days, Tatiana would "treat" Natalia. Gone were the fruit salads and smoothies for breakfast to make room for the pastries, bacon, cheesy grits, and sausage. Their dinners changed from grilled chicken over dry greens to bags full of fast-food burgers and greasy pizza. Natalia loved the splurge, but the joy was short-lived. When she thought she was being treated to something special, she loved the food. But, when she realized what Tatiana was really doing, trying to fatten Natalia up to make herself feel better, the food just disgusted her. To this day, she still craves sweets, but the idea of fast food brings back bad memories.

They pulled over and into the drive-thru. Natalia, with her head still against the frame, closed her eyes and breathed in the fresh air, almost able to taste the French fries through the smells coming out of the restaurant. She listened to Daniel anxiously, placing his order.

"I'll have a cheeseburger with fries and a chocolate milkshake." He said, staring straight ahead and waiting for a reply.

The woman in the car behind them beeped, and when she noticed that Daniel was ignoring her, the petite blonde woman exited her car and walked up to his window.

Irritated that no one replied to his order and this woman was now approaching, he said, as condescendingly as possible, "What can I do for you?"

"You need to pull up," said the woman in a sweet, southern accent, oblivious to his rude tone.

"Thank you for your concern," he answered sarcastically. "But I am waiting for them to confirm my order."

At that moment, watching the woman's half-smile creep across her cheek as she muttered, "Bless your heart."

Natalia realized the woman was not oblivious to his rudeness; she was just trying not to embarrass him.

Natalia leaned across Daniel, looked knowingly at the woman, waved, and said, "Thank you."

"What are you..." Daniel started, frustrated.

"Just pull up to the speaker." Natalia interrupted.

Daniel gave her an angry look. "Don't embarrass me in front of..."

"Daniel," she said calmly, trying to keep him from escalating, "you're talking into the trash can. Pull up to the speaker."

Daniel quickly looked out the window and realized his mistake. Standing in front of the menu was a bin with an extra-long adaptor allowing people to throw garbage into it from their car window with less of a chance of missing the mark. The speaker was on the *other* side of the menu. He cleared his throat and slowly pulled up about six more feet to the speaker.

"How can I help you?" the friendly, disembodied voice said.

Natalia bit down on her bottom lip and tried not to laugh. He was obviously not in a good mood, and now, he was fuming. His ears were such a deep red she wondered if flames would soon shoot out. He repeated the order he previously relayed to the trash can, then pulled up to the window, still not making eye contact with Natalia.

He reached out the window and handed the teenager at the window his credit card. Since Daniel would not smile, Natalia leaned over and smiled at the kid.

When he reached out of the window to give Daniel his card back, Daniel snatched it from the boy's hand and said, "Thank you." And drove off without looking up.

Natalia just stared at him. She was amazed at how quickly he could lose his cool. Not only had he talked down to the woman who was trying to help, he felt insulted by Natalia for correcting him and took it all out on the poor kid working the drive-thru.

It was only a few weeks ago when she made weed-killer brownies for a chauvinistic and rude old man she met through Bunny's contacts. What made some men think they were above others? Certainly, in both situations, it was not masculinity. Daniel was tall and built but was not someone she would describe as masculine. They seemed determined to take their station in life at the top of the food chain.

She leaned back against the door frame, again feeling the wind in her hair, and wondered how long it would take him to notice that he drove off without the food.

THe SMeLL OF Fear

Daniel directed the car back onto the highway, heading in the opposite direction from where he had planned to go. He had hoped to hit the outlet stores and spend time with Natalia, but he couldn't relax. He was more concerned with what the person next to him was doing than the cars on the road. He was hungry, frustrated, and needed to get all of these suspicions about Natalia off his chest. He pulled off at the next exit and then onto an unpaved road. The gravel crunched underneath the tires as he pulled to a stop and turned off the car. He was unsure how to start, but the longer he stared at his steering wheel with Natalia's eyes boring through him, the more anxious he became.

"Daniel, what's going on?" she asked with undisguised confusion. "I know you are nervous." She paused and took a long sniff of the air. "And scared. Daniel, why are you scared?"

Something about the way she asked frightened him even more. How did she know that he was scared, and why the hell was she smelling the air?

He took his hands off the wheel and wiped his sweaty palms on his pants. He looked straight ahead, unable to even glance in Natalia's direction. Focusing on a large knot in the tree about twenty yards in front of the car was the only way for him to calm down.

"Look, Natalia. I am not sure how to say this," he began with a sigh, his eyes still avoiding hers. "I know... that... uh... you haven't been completely honest with me, and I can't continue to live with you knowing what you've been up to."

He pried his eyes off the tree and finally worked up the nerve to look at her. First, he looked to her lap, where her hands were folded and unmoving, then up to her eyes. She looked at him sympathetically and with a touch of pity. Or was that guilt?

"I'm sorry, Daniel. I didn't want you to find out. I hoped to protect you from all of this. But I guess it was bound to happen, eventually. If it makes you feel any better, they're horrible humans and really annoying." She laughed to herself momentarily before composing herself.

Daniel stared at her with his mouth agape. "What? What?" He couldn't get the words out. Who's horrible? Stuart and Bunny? What the hell is going on, Natalia?"

"Shit," Natalia said, glancing out the window, looking around them as if checking for on-lookers. "I guess I completely misunderstood what you were saying. I thought you found out what Stuart and I have been doing." She looked back at Daniel. "I did it for you, you know... for your career."

"Don't say another word. Just knowing could get me in a lot of trouble. I don't want to know anything more."

"You know, you're right. I don't think you want to know. Maybe we should just drop it altogether. Let's go shopping, or maybe we can go to grab a drink somewhere. What do you say?"

He was keenly aware that she had shifted back into fake, sweet Natalia mode. Her voice was slightly higher, her head was tilted downward, making her eyes look larger than normal, and her posture more lax and immature than her previous, erect power position. This wasn't her. Why was she acting? What else was she hiding?

"No. I want to get back to the city. I will come back and get some shopping done another day. Heck, maybe I will just order some things online. Look, I will drop you off first, then take the car back," he said decisively. "I need some time to think."

Daniel restarted the car and slowly pulled back onto the exit ramp. His hands were still sweaty, and his fingers started to cramp from the intensity with which he grabbed the steering wheel. He looked straight ahead, maneuvering to get back on the highway and going back to where they came from. He felt beads of sweat pop up on his brow and upper lip. He wanted to wipe it off, but he didn't want her to see him sweat. He could feel her eyes on him still. *Why was she staring at him*? He desperately wanted her to look out of her window so he could wipe his face on his shoulder.

In what seemed like slow motion, a giant sweat droplet fell from his forehead and landed, making a wet circle on the crotch of his khaki pants. When he wondered if she saw, he heard Natalia sigh audibly, saying, "I can smell your fear, Daniel. Get a grip on yourself."

***

In one brief outing with her brother, Natalia knew everything had changed. The siblings would never be able to go back to the way things were. She let her guard down at some point, and he saw through to her true colors. How had she slipped up and how much did he actually know?

Natalia was unsure if they could co-exist as roommates or even as friends. The one thing she knew for sure was that their world had forever changed.

DO THE RIGHT THING

Daniel paced the same path back and forth in front of his couch. His heart was racing, but not from exertion. With every glance around the condo, a new reminder of Natalia popped up. She packed her bag and left earlier in the morning, yet it already felt empty without her. He was so happy when she came into his life, but lately, he felt he never really knew her. He stopped pacing and pressed his pointer fingers into his temples, and pinched his eyes closed. How had he not seen what was going on? Now that Natalia had unintentionally come clean, it all made sense, even back to that first night at the club.

He remembered the way Stuart looked at Natalia like there was some odd connection between them. It was almost like he was intrigued by her, entertained by her peculiar ways. Then all that time passed after Daniel's confrontation with Stuart at the club when Natalia supposedly went to the bathroom. What was she doing that whole time? Of course, it makes sense to him now that Stuart has apologized. She must have made him an offer he couldn't refuse. From the beginning, she had masterminded everything from his dream job to her employment with Bunny. That made him think of Bunny. From what he knew of her, she was beautiful and very kind. Did she know what they were up to? Did she have any idea what those two were capable of? How could the sweet girl who just appeared in his life barter her soul just so Daniel could have a job?

The thought made him sick, and he sunk down against the wall to the floor. It only made sense that Daniel would have to tell someone. Should he tell Bunny? What about the stockholders? Did he need to tell the board so it didn't look like he was somehow involved in their scheme?

Daniel sat up straight and gently banged the back of his head against the wall over and over several times before stopping and dropping his head into his hands. He knew she was not the innocent girl he had made her out to be, but he never would've imagined that she could commit such evil acts. Maybe he should blame their dad for that. Maybe growing up with an absent father who abandoned her mother over and over wreaks havoc on one's moral compass.

He let go of his head, slapped his palms against the floor, and pushed himself up. His mother taught him very young to make a pros and cons list when faced with a tough decision. He stood, brushed off his pants, and walked to the kitchen. Pulling open one of the drawers on the island, Daniel pulled out a sheet of lined paper and a pencil.

He made two columns, pros and cons, and above them, he wrote down a question.

First, the pros... Directly under the PROS header, he wrote 1. CYA. If the board found out, he didn't want to be culpable. Hell, he didn't even want Bunny to know he had any idea.

When he reread what he wrote, he felt awash with guilt. Natalia had done all of this for him, and here he was just trying to cover his own ass, so under CONS, he wrote BETRAYAL OF NATALIA.

While he was on that thought, he had another selfish con: COULD LOSE MY JOB.

His stomach was in knots. This was turning out to be a lot harder than he expected. After close to an hour of writing, erasing, moving items from one column to another, and jumping up to pace the room, he wrote the last pro down and felt there was no turning back.

PROS

    1. CYA

    2. MAY SAVE MY JOB

    3. BUNNY SHOULD KNOW

    4. IT'S THE RIGHT THING

CONS

    1. BETRAYAL OF NATALIA

    2. COULD LOSE MY JOB

    3. BUNNY COULD BE HURT

    4. MAY GET BLACKBALLED

Daniel sighed deeply as he laid the list on the kitchen counter, absent-mindedly drawing a big circle around 4. IT'S THE RIGHT THING. That settled things in his mind. He would confront the two of them together and allow them to come clean on their own. That seemed fair and made him feel better about bringing things out into the open. If he gave them a chance to do it on their own, it only seemed fair that they would give him a break. He wasn't the one in the wrong, after all.

It should be easy enough to organize a time to talk to them since Natalia was staying with Stuart and Bunny since she moved out earlier in the day. Daniel scoffed loudly to himself and shuddered as he picked up his phone to make the call. He decided it was best to arrange it with Stuart. Somehow, the thought of talking to Natalia right now disgusted him. As if second-guessing himself, he grabbed a red pen off the counter and added one more bullet point to the list.

THE FOUNTAIN OF YOUTH

Natalia had plans to meet Francisco at the coffee shop. She was excited to see him again, mostly because of the way their last encounter ended. Her pent-up sexual tension, combined with her stress over what was going on with Daniel, made for a very explosive situation.

The bell on the door jangled as she walked into the corner cafe. When she didn't see Francisco, she headed back to the bathroom. She could categorize each person she walked past without knowing them. She hadn't lived in the city long, but she'd already found there were certain types that frequented coffee shops. First, there was *earpiece businessman* who could probably take his call elsewhere but likes to look important. Next, there is *exhausted new mom* mindlessly pushing her stroller back and forth while blankly staring at the wall for a few precious minutes until her baby wakes up crying, and she has to leave. Then, there are two separate *better than online dating* singles, eyeing each other over their phone or laptop, pretending to be busy but really just there to meet someone. Lastly, there was a table of *pretending to be grown-up teenagers*, all sipping their coffees with caffeine they certainly don't need, looking at their phones, and only talking to each other when they wanted to share a funny meme.

When Natalia made it to the back of the cafe, she found the bathroom door locked. She stood, leaning against the wall opposite the bathroom door, and waited for the occupant to exit. A man walked past her, who, at first glance, she thought was Francisco. He was young and handsome, but he was carrying a large vat of coffee, and last she checked, Francisco didn't work there. Or, maybe that explained why he was late. She chuckled to herself as she watched his tight ass walk through the backroom door.

"Do you look at my ass that way?" said Francisco's sexy voice.

Natalia turned around, shocked as she hadn't heard anyone walk up, then almost at the same time, a woman emerged from the bathroom, not fitting any coffee shop stereotypes. This woman donned an outfit more suited for an evening at the club. Her hair was a bit of a rat's nest, and her makeup was streaked and worn. Then it hit her. This woman was on her walk of shame from a one-night stand. Either she is on her way home or maybe stepped out to get coffee as code for not wanting to use the dude's bathroom.

Natalia recalled a story her mom told her when she was younger. Tatiana had been on a spring break trip with one girl and at least ten boys. There was nothing romantic between the girls and any of the boys, but the girls were still uncomfortable using the bathroom around them. So, every morning, Tatiana and her friend would drive to a local attraction to use their lobby bathroom. Boys weren't allowed to know that women took shits, too. Tatiana would laugh about it, and every time she needed to use the bathroom, she would announce, "I'm heading to the Fountain of Youth."

The little hussy gave Francisco a good eye-fuck before resuming her walk of shame.

"You gave her an eyeful, that's for sure," Natalia said, taking in how handsome he was just wearing a simple white tee and jeans.

Catching the door to the bathroom before it closed, she grabbed Francisco by a belt loop and pulled him in with her. She locked the door and leaned in for a long, passionate kiss.

Pressing her body against his, she could already feel an erection through his pants.

With her lips still pursed, she opened her eyes, looking around, realizing how disgusting it was to be making out in a public bathroom.

As if they both realized it at the same time, they looked at each other and said, "Nope." And quickly exited the bathroom.

They threw the door open so fast that they almost ran into Francisco's look-alike, who hurried by with a new vat of coffee, muttering, "Well, there goes our Grade-A rating," in a strong Mexican accent.

Completely forgetting about her need to use the bathroom, Natalia sat at an empty table next to the teenage texters. At least the spot would be quiet.

Francisco joined her with two coffees a few minutes later. "You seem very stressed."

"I don't really want to get into it, but it's my brother." She took a long, loud sip watching the teens for any reaction at all. Would they hear her long, obnoxious slurp, or would they be too engrossed in their phones to notice? When she saw not one person look up, she turned back to Francisco and continued, "It's just my brother. He thinks he is smarter than he is. I don't like it when people get all high and mighty."

Francisco was a good listener. Rather than trying to fix her problem or explain away what was bothering her, he leaned forward, listening attentively, and sipping his coffee, waited for her to continue.

"He doesn't know me," Natalia said, placing both of her hands in her lap and looking down at them.

"Do I know you?" Francisco questioned.

Natalia sighed deeply and raised her eyes to meet his. "You don't know everything there is to know about me, but you know me better than Daniel does." She raised her eyes up to the left and then continued. "Well, maybe it's not so much that you know me better. It's that you understand me. You get me." Then her eyes fixed back on Francisco's deep, brown eyes, and feeling insecure, she bit her lip and added, "I think."

Francisco sat back in his chair, not taking his eyes off Natalia but helping himself to more of his coffee. "I see you," he began, which relaxed Natalia slightly. "I have seen two sides of you, but I only believe one is you. That Natalia is the one I am drawn to."

Thinking back to their previous interactions, she asked, "What is the other me?"

He smiled. "I only met your brother once, but I noticed that your body became rigid the second he walked in. You became an actor on stage, making sure to say the exact, scripted line, careful of your every movement. I don't pretend to understand it, but I see it."

Francisco was right. She had been playing a mental chess game since she met Daniel, and it was exhausting pretending to be someone she wasn't.

Francisco's kind words touched her. Her chest felt warm, and her tummy tingled with butterflies. She inhaled the clean scent of fresh laundry, making her smile. She pretended to take a sip of coffee and took extra time with her nose in the empty mug, trying to place the smell. She was almost certain the smell was coming from her. For her entire life, she never recognized her own smell. Kind of like how people don't seem to be able to smell their own body odor or bad breath. The smell was overpowering, and with each tickle in her tummy that made her fidget in her seat, she realized it must be her. What was this scent that brought her so much joy?

Francisco must have noticed her being deep in thought, and rather than interrupt or even ask her what she was thinking, he simply placed his large, smooth hands on her knee, causing her butterflies to shoot from her little baby toe all the way up to the top of her scalp.

THe COnFROnTaTion

Since her uncomfortable trip to the suburbs with Daniel, Natalia had been staying with Bunny and Stuart, hoping the space would keep him from asking questions or digging any deeper into their conversation in the car. Out of sight, out of mind, she hoped. Natalia padded out to the living room from the guest room in which she was staying to find Bunny with her headphones on, grinning at something on her phone, and Stuart leaning on the side of the couch, looking out the window, seemingly deep in thought.

Natalia plopped on the couch between the two but neither moved nor said a thing. It was strangely comfortable for her amongst these two. She felt she could be completely herself, talk with them about anything or sit in total silence and never feel out of place. After relaying the news of Daniel finding out more than she intended, they were both surprisingly calm. She was unsure if they overestimated Daniel's ability to go with the flow or underestimated his ability to stand up to them, but either way, they didn't see the problem. Natalia, on the other hand, was a ball of nerves. Not only did she feel that she was losing her brother, but she felt that Daniel could really hurt them if he shared everything he found out.

Following Stuart's gaze, Natalia stared out the window, but on a dreary, cloudy day like it was, nothing was visible. She wondered what he was thinking about and whether he thought she had failed them. Natalia sniffed the air to get a sense of his current state of mind but got nothing.

Then the phone rang. Stuart and Natalia both jumped and looked down at their phones on the coffee table, while Bunny ignored or didn't even hear the rings through her headphones. The call was to Stuart. As they reached at the same time, however, it was visible to them both that the caller was Daniel or Daniel-san, as Stuart had him listed in his caller ID. Natalia bit her lower lip as Stuart moved to pick up the phone, then she leaned back against the sofa, crossed her arms, and began chewing on her fingernails.

"Hey, Daniel-san. How's it going?" Stuart asked in such an upbeat manner that it was hard to imagine he knew anything was up.

His smile dropped slightly, but he nodded, threw in a few *uh huh's*, and disconnected. Bunny must've seen Natalia's nervous fidgeting because when Stuart put the phone back on the table, Bunny's headphones were off, and she was staring, waiting for an update.

"Well, that was Daniel," he began. Natalia rolled her eyes, wondering why he didn't just skip that part, but she held her tongue.

"He said he's taken some time to clear his head and wants to come over tomorrow evening to meet in private." Stuart sighed, looking on edge for the first time. "If this is him after he calmed down, I can't imagine what he must've been like in the car... in a confined space together, finding out something like that..." Stuart began to trail off, and Natalia and Bunny exchanged nervous glances.

"He sounded like he was going to stroke it!"

"I think you mean stroke out, dear," Bunny corrected without batting an eye.

"Exactly!" Stuart jumped up. "Anyway, he said he had been putting together the pieces and doesn't feel that he can keep it to himself but first wants to give us an opportunity to explain." Then, drifting off to another thought, Stuart mumbled to himself, "Which makes me wonder how much he really does know, because if he knows, why would he put himself in that si—"

"Stuart, sweetheart," Bunny started as if onto an idea. "Did you ever search him?"

"What? No," he said, taking offense. "You know I don't swing that way."

This time Bunny sighed and walked over to his side. "Did you ever search his background? Did you ever look for something, anything in his past that can be used against him, to at least keep him quiet if it comes to that?"

Bunny insecurely glanced in the direction of the couch to see if Natalia took offense as an afterthought, but Natalia simply nodded, waiting for an answer.

"No. Nothing. Either he is clean, or his rich-ass parents got him out of trouble." Stuart looked back out the window at the swirling clouds. "Anyway, I'm not sure that is the best way to handle Daniel. Give me some time to think about it, and we will see what he says tomorrow."

He turned to Bunny, saying, "I don't think you should be here, or at least not in the room. If he doesn't know you are involved, there is no reason to give him that information now." Turning his eyes to Natalia, still curled up on the couch, chewing on her cuticles, having already torn through the nails. "You should be here. There's strength in numbers, and he already knows we're both involved."

Stuart looked back and forth between the two women looking for some sort of acknowledgment or agreement. Both women nodded, which seemed to be good enough for him.

Natalia stood and quietly said, "Excuse me. I need some time alone." Then she walked back to the guest room.

THE INTERVENTION

Wracked with guilt, Natalia sat on the large, soft chaise lounge, looking out the window. She stared out at the dark and stormy clouds because she couldn't stand to look at the elegant room that surrounded her. She had gone so far as to strip off the clothes she was wearing that Bunny had bought for her on their last shopping trip. Stuart and Bunny gave her a chance. They gave her a purpose. They took her in and fully had her back. They didn't try to change her. Natalia was not *weird* to them, and now Natalia's slip-up could cost them everything. Why did she open her big mouth? Even if Daniel thought he knew something, why didn't she deny, deny, deny? Certainly, she knew him well enough by now to know he would never go along with their plan. He would never accept her for who she really is. He would certainly not be complemented by her feeling what she had done was for his benefit.

With tears flooding her eyes, she could hardly make out the box in the corner of her temporary room. She blinked away the tears and made her way over to the decorative box that sat on the ground, no bigger than a shoe box. The colors were bright, and the designs were meant to inspire happiness with a random assortment of flowers, stars, cats, and smiling suns. But the box did not bring her happiness. She only felt cold when she looked at the cheesy yet beautiful box that held death within. In it, she kept any and all remnants of medications and poisons she had obtained illegally from Francisco.

She remembered when her mother gave her the box as a gift. Natalia was only five and had accompanied Tatiana to a casino when the babysitter fell through. Following another disappointment from Natalia's father, Tatiana took the recent payout he sent instead of visiting. She bought the box to carry the cash and vowed to take it all to the casino and either become a millionaire or blow it all, just to spite him. Tatiana always felt she had a special gift when it came to reading people, especially in poker. But, to her amazement, Natalia could tell who had a good hand and who was bluffing based on their smell. Once the money was all converted to chips, Tatiana gave her the box.

"Natalia, my sweet angel. You have an amazing gift, and it would be wrong not to use it."

She felt so special and would do anything to keep her mother happy. She sat by her mom's side at the table and would pull her ear closest to Tatiana when someone was bluffing. Unfortunately, management kicked them out before they could rake in any good money.

"What are you kicking us out for?" Tatiana screamed, making a scene, feeling like she was going to miss out on her big payday.

"We know you are cheating. We haven't figured out exactly how yet, but it is crystal clear that you are. However, without proof, we only have you as a suspected cheater, which in itself is grounds for us to ban you. But, if you want something formal, minors are not allowed at the tables. I have no idea why someone didn't stop you earlier," the head of security explained calmly, without emotion, and quite clearly.

"It's not my fault someone let her in? I didn't know that was a rule. She didn't say a word the whole time. I don't see how she could possibly be a problem," Tatiana said, continuing to argue to no avail.

The large man smiled down at Natalia and opened the back door for them to exit. "She seems like a very special young lady." Then, looking back at Tatiana said, "But, either way, you are now banned from our casino, and your picture is being distributed to any other casino in our network as a possible cheater. Have a nice night." He shut the door and left them standing right outside, staring at the cold, dark steel doors.

"This is all your fault!" Tatiana yelled. "All you had to do was sit there quietly and signal me, but you were so obvious they caught on. No minors, huh? They didn't say a word until you started yanking on your ear, and we started winning."

The wonderful feeling she had when her mother appreciated and wanted to nurture her gift was gone. There was only one other time when she felt good about what she could do when her mother sent her to a shrink as a teenager. Tatiana's intention was to "cure" her crazy, or at least suppress her weirdness, so it was less evident. However, to Natalia's surprise, the psychologist had no intention of doing that at all.

"So, Natalia. From what your mother tells me, you can smell things most people cannot, like feelings or personalities. Is that correct?"

Ms. Jen was tall, thin, and approachable, but Natalia was nervous and didn't want to be there. She nodded but continued to look down at her hands that were clenched on her lap.

"It sounds to me like you have superpowers," the friendly voice said.

Natalia looked up quickly, wondering if she was being mocked, only to see Ms. Jen smiling at her as if she had just made an amazing discovery. "I think you are a very special girl who can do things that most people cannot. That makes you different but not inferior. Unique, not odd. No, in fact, your abilities are quite remarkable. I would love to meet with you every week and explore your gifts. It would be research for me, so you wouldn't have to pay, but my hope would be that any information we gain from our meetings will be beneficial to you, as well. The more you know about your gift, the easier it will be for you to control."

Needless to say, Tatiana wasn't pleased with the therapist's enthusiasm and encouragement of the one thing she hoped to rid Natalia of. She never saw Ms. Jen again, nor any other therapist, psychiatrist, psychologist, or counselor for that matter.

Her mother, though a monster of a bitch, had been her entire life. With her gone, she thought Daniel would be her family and would love her and accept her for the way she was, unlike her dear old mom. Nothing had turned out the way she anticipated. Now, she doesn't have her mom, and Daniel disapproves of her just as much as her mom ever did. Natalia didn't feel that she had the choice to go back and pretend to be someone else. Not anymore. That ship had sailed. She blew her shot with Daniel, and he would never see her the same way again.

Her life was ruined. She should open up that box of death and treat herself to a large enough dose of whatever she grabbed first to allow herself to simply fall asleep and never wake up. For a moment, she reflected on the disgusting scene she left behind when she used the blue crystal substance, whose remnants were still inside the box, to kill a large and very unpleasant woman. Maybe if the woman hadn't been so much of a bitch, Natalia would feel some remorse, but as of now, she just made a mental note not to go out like that. Pissing oneself upon death is not a dignified way to leave this earth.

She felt no need to torture herself as penance for her sins but couldn't think of one reason to go on. She had nothing. She had no one.

Natalia heard laughter through the walls and wondered what Stuart and Bunny would think of her if she took the easy way out. They would probably love to get her out of their life, out of their house. What a nice clean way to wrap things up for them. Daniel could be manipulated, no doubt. But, to rid themselves of their smoking gun would clean the slate for them. Plus, they had to be getting sick of having her around their house all of the time. And Bunny could actually get a real assistant. She could certainly afford it, and she wasn't getting anything out of Natalia. The ruse left Bunny to fend for herself, not that she ever complained.

While thinking of Stuart and Bunny and all that they'd done for her, her crying intensified. She sat on the floor in a straddle and pulled the box nearer to her as if taking one more step closer to ending her life. Natalia shuddered as her sobs wracked her body. The emotions were desperate to escape, shaking her body uncontrollably and causing goose bumps to rise up on her skin. She tried with every ounce of her will to hold back the tears and, more importantly, to remain quiet. If she could hear their laughs, certainly they could hear her pathetic wailing.

Another loud, boisterous laugh filtered through the wall, and Natalia felt her heart break a little bit more. She could just picture Bunny's contagious and genuine smile. Had she ruined the lives of these two amazing people who took her in and didn't expect her to be anything other than her true self? For a moment, the hysterical crying turned into hysterical laughter as she thought of Stuart, his stupid "You Do You" mantra, and how he was so genuine that he actually practiced what he preached. He lived that way, and he encouraged others to do the same.

The laughter and voices were getting closer, and the soft, graceful sound of Bunny's fluffy slippers could be heard getting louder, swishing along the tile floors. Natalia quickly wiped her snotty nose on her bare arm and rubbed her hands over her face to wipe away the stray tears. She knew she couldn't lock them out, it was their home, after all, but she couldn't let them see her like this either, adding to the heavy burden they already carried.

The knock on the door alerted her to Bunny's presence, and Natalia was thankful that she hadn't turned the lights on as the evening approached. Bunny pushed the door open, saying, "Girl, we need you. We are pulling random *Would You Rather* questions from the internet. It's hilarious. Maria is mixing up a batch of her margaritas," she said, emphasizing the word margaritas in a very bad, but adorable, Spanish accent. "And we decided we really need you in there. Everything is more fun with you."

Natalia watched from under her swollen and heavy eyelids as Bunny's expression changed from pure happiness to extreme concern as she noticed Natalia sitting in the dark on the floor in her bra and panties, legs spread next to her death box.

She couldn't remember ever telling Bunny about the death box, but like Natalia's mind, Bunny knew there were things Natalia kept that were private and even dangerous. Not to mention that no one was allowed to clean her room for the safety of others.

"What are you doing?" Bunny asked softly but with a sense of urgency.

Natalia sniffed, wiped a bit more snot onto her already crusty forearm, and stared at the box.

When Bunny started to push the door open farther and enter the room, Natalia yelled, "STOP!" She composed herself after seeing the stunned look on Bunny's face and continued, "I don't want you to see me like this."

"Okay, I won't come in, but I'm going to sit right here at the door, okay?"

Natalia said nothing but nodded her head reluctantly in the realization that it was Bunny's house, and she could really do whatever she wanted.

"So, what's going on?" Bunny asked, this time with less panic in her voice. It was as if the initial shock of what she saw had worn off, and now she was in crisis mode. She looked like she fully prepared herself to hold it together and talk Natalia down from whatever was happening. Maybe she had missed her calling as a social worker or crisis intervention specialist. But Natalia knew that Bunny couldn't help her. No one could help her. As her mom said, *No one would ever understand her, no one would ever care for her; she was just too weird.*

"What's in the box?" Bunny asked, sitting on her knees, looking anxious to crawl into the room but holding herself back out of respect.

"Things that you don't need to concern yourself with. It doesn't matter," Natalia answered so quietly she was unsure if Bunny would even hear her.

"Can I hold it for you?" Bunny asked like she was offering to carry in the groceries.

"No!" Natalia snapped. "You should go. Don't come in here. Stay away from me. I'll figure out a way out of this. I don't want to hurt you and Stuart. You're all I love in this world."

She said it before the thought processed, almost shocking herself. But that was it, wasn't it? These were the only two people she had ever met in her whole life who not only accepted her for who she was but loved her inspite of it. They weren't family, but they loved her like no family ever had.

Bunny lowered her voice and sat against the wall, saying, "We love you, too. You are a part of our life now; we don't want that to change. You have changed us, and I truly believe there is nothing that we cannot do if we stick together."

"But this whole mess with Daniel..." Natalia trailed off, looking back down at the box. Rather than jumping in, Bunny patiently waited for her to be ready to continue.

"This whole thing with Daniel is all my fault. I wasn't ready. As my eighth-grade social studies teacher used to say, 'He caught me with my britches down and my butt cheeks flapping in the breeze.' I didn't think he suspected anything, and I was caught off guard. I've thought of a million other ways to handle that conversation better."

Bunny kept so quiet that Natalia had to look up to see if she was still there. She was, and she looked at her not with a look of pity but of love, and the strong smell of baby powder filled the room. That was new to her. She was unfamiliar with that smell. But whatever it was, she was pleased. Bunny did not pity her, she didn't feel sorry for her, and it was clear, even in her silence, that she was not going to let her wallow in her guilt either.

***

She remembered a young girl she knew briefly as a teen. Her name was Foster, and she lived just out of the city on a farm. Her parents drove over an hour each way to bring her to school each day. Foster was unapologetically unique. She cared little for style but somehow always ended up looking badass. Best yet, she had a pig she dressed up in a tutu named Bacon.

Unlike every other kid in middle school, she never felt the pressure to conform to the latest trend.

People were unkind to her, but she didn't care. She flaunted her differences with pride. Her mother, however, heard the things people were saying about her daughter and immediately pulled her out of school and resumed homeschooling. Natalia hadn't thought of her much since, and thinking about her now made her wonder what Foster was up to. There wasn'tt a purer human on the planet. Of that, she was sure. She was likely running a sustainable co-op to provide fresh and healthy produce to the underprivileged or maybe even a shelter for neglected pets of all types. Natalia actually believed, out of all the people she'd met in her life, that Foster was the only person who truly made the world a better place.

Until Bunny. Was Bunny the new Foster? Though Foster's rural exterior was different from the plastic exterior Bunny wore so well, they were both smart and genuine. The world was full of self-righteous assholes, judgmental pricks, and annoying wastes of space, but just one Foster... just one Bunny... made the world tolerable, and those people less of a stain.

***

Stuart's footsteps could be heard clomping down the hall along with his humming what sounded like a game show theme song. The two women stared at each other, neither moving as Stuart rounded the corner holding two huge salt-rimmed glasses full to the brim with frozen Margaritas and topped with a small red fruit Natalia didn't recognize.

"One for you," he said, handing Bunny a glass and kissing her lightly on the top of her head. "And one for you," he said obliviously, walking boldly into the dark room and handing a glass to Natalia. He turned to walk away, not mentioning the strange situation he had just walked in on or the fact Natalia was near nude. On his way out, he said, "I just pulled up two more pages of questions, ladies. This is about to get cray." He resumed his humming as he continued down the hall.

"I talked Maria into making nachos too," he yelled in a high-pitch, giddy voice, sounding like a kid getting their favorite meal after months of requests.

Natalia looked from the spot where Stuart had left her sight and back to Bunny, who just looked at her lovingly. She wondered if this was what it was supposed to feel like to have a mother, to have someone who loved you unconditionally, despite your flaws. Was this what it felt like to have someone who would rather accept your differences than have you be anyone other than your true self? Maybe this is what it was like to have a caring dad... awkward and unsure of how to handle girl problems, but there for you anyway.

"Come on. Let's go play," Bunny said, standing and offering her hand.

Natalia grabbed it and stood with a weak smile. Bunny pulled her into a tight hug, which made Natalia cry even harder. She never understood, until now, what it was like to cry out of happiness rather than only having tears of sadness and anger. She was happy and loved; in this moment, she knew she would do anything for Bunny, a mother, a sister, and a best friend, all wrapped up in a beautiful package.

Natalia stepped back from the embrace and grabbed Bunny's hand as she made to walk out of the room, but Bunny didn't move.

Natalia stopped and stared, only then noticing she was still not dressed when Bunny gave her a once over.

"Oh, yeah, clothes." Natalia giggled, feeling so much joy that she felt it had to get out somehow. "I'll meet you out there."

She knew that Bunny trusted her because she simply nodded and left the room while Natalia threw on jeans and a T-shirt and carefully placed the box up high on the top shelf of her closet.

Finally, appropriately clothed, Natalia walked out to find Bunny standing behind Stuart, seated in the middle of the long dining table. His elbows were propped on the table, and his fingers pressed against each other, resting under his chin. He would've looked like a mob boss without the nacho cheese on his cheek and the chunk of salsa hanging from his chin.

A slow grin crept across his face as he said, "Ladies, I have a plan… and I think you're gonna like it."

THe Proposal

The house phone rang and was promptly answered by Stuart. By his curt but polite response, Natalia surmised that the call was from the doorman to request visitor access to their private elevator. It was 5:50 p.m., and they expected Daniel at 6:00 p.m. He was nothing if not prompt. She stood on the threshold of her room to the main living area, unsure if she could take the next step toward confrontation. She was brave and calm in stressful situations, but now, she was shaking, biting her nails, and plucking at her eyebrows.

Stuart passed her door on the way to the elevator and saw her standing there.

"Hiding won't help. Daniel knows enough to be a problem. We need to find out exactly what he knows and make him a deal he can't refuse. There is no reason to assume he won't want in on our plan, right?" Stuart said confidently.

Natalia was not nearly as confident, however. Daniel may not know the real Natalia, but she felt certain she knew the real Daniel. He was honest, almost to a fault, and even if he agreed to keep a secret, he had an uncanny way of having loose lips. As awkward as he could be in social situations, she couldn't even imagine how he would cover up anything that slipped out.

"Go to the bathroom, splash some water on your face, and pull your shit together," he said in a rough but caring way.

Natalia knew she was still a mess from the previous night. She was so close to walking over the edge, but instead of giving her a push, Stuart and Bunny pulled her back to safety with an unrelenting hug. She owed them both. The next half hour was going to decide all of their futures.

"I'll just freshen up and throw on some makeup, okay?" Natalia said in reply just as she heard the elevator door ding.

Daniel was here, and she was falling apart.

Stuart looked at her with a sad half-smile. "You do you," he said, going to the foyer to meet Daniel.

She knew he was worried about her. She knew that both he and Bunny truly cared about her. In fact, she had come to realize that her relationship with Stuart had been all she had hoped she would have with Daniel and more. The brother she got wasn't the brother she needed, but the brother she needed was the friend who was there. Things just worked out in quite an unexpected way, somehow.

Once in the bathroom, Natalia ran a brush through her hair, dotted some concealer under her eyes, and powdered her face. She had hoped that was all she needed, but looking in the mirror, she looked washed out. She swiped on some mascara and added a neutral lip gloss and felt better.

The static was thick in the air, and her brush didn't help. She quickly pulled her hair back into a ponytail, thinking how difficult this conversation would be if she tried to be serious with her hair sticking up all over her head.

Natalia looked in the mirror one final time and gave herself a whispering pep talk. "You can do this. You're a badass. He's your brother and will do what you ask. He doesn't want to hurt you. You are just different from each other. You have people who love you, so you don't need him. He's not all you have. Be strong."

When she joined Stuart and Daniel in the living room, Stuart was sitting leisurely on the couch, sipping a cocktail while Daniel stood by the wall of windows, pacing back and forth. When he saw her walk in, he showed a glimmer of excitement followed by his back stiffening up and his smile dropping, as if only just remembering what he was there for. He resumed his pacing, but this time with added knuckle cracking.

To break the uncomfortable silence that followed the loud and obnoxious cracking, Stuart asked Natalia to sit down, which helped her uncertainty of whether she should go to Daniel and hug him. She sat, not taking her eyes off her brother.

"Natalia, would you like a drink? I offered one to Daniel, but he isn't interested," Stuart said lightheartedly.

"No, thank you," she replied, trying to swallow down the lump in her throat, creating a slight tickle and making her cough ironically after refusing a drink. Her eyes watered as she tried to suck as much saliva as she could into her cheeks so she could swallow her spit and soothe her cough. She could feel the color on her face as she fought against the automatic reflex.

Daniel moved to lean against a wall but wasn't looking and missed. He stumbled clumsily but caught himself before falling. He straightened himself and spoke as if nothing had happened.

"I know what's been going on. I want no part of it and will not go down with you," he said in an outburst, becoming even redder in the face.

"Daniel, relax, man," Stuart said, standing, likely to give himself a more powerful position. "I think I speak for both of us," he began, gesturing to Natalia. "When I say that, we are both very thankful that you came here so we can clear the air. I can tell you that both of us have worked entirely with your best interest at heart."

Natalia fought not to roll her eyes, feeling Stuart was pouring it on a bit thick. But one look at Daniel and she remembered that this was his boss. This was the guy that he had looked up to from afar for years. That compliment, though cheesy and not completely accurate, was precisely what Daniel wanted to hear. That was the kind of ass-kissing he just ate up.

Daniel stopped his aimless wandering and took a seat on the big, fluffy chair in the corner and sank in deep. He didn't fight the awkward and less-than-powerful posture it gave him. He looked resigned. He looked beat.

"I believe this can all be cleared up and straightened out. Since I know you don't want to be a part of this, you may want to tender your resignation. All I ask of you is for one week. One week to change your mind." Stuart watched Daniel for any kind of agreement. When he received none, he continued, "In the meantime, I would like to send you and Natalia to my place at a resort in Puerto Bahia." The mention of vacation seemed to get Daniel's attention, so Stuart went on, "The two of you can leave town for a..." He paused and began gesturing finger quotes. "Family emergency or dead aunt or something like that. You both relax, spend time together, meet the locals, and have fun. When you return, hopefully, you will have decided to stay on, with a hefty retention bonus, of course. But if not, I will accept your resignation, advance your year-end bonus and send you on your way to bigger and better places with a glowing recommendation. One week. I'm only asking for one week to think things through before you do anything rash."

"So. Um. You'll just send us away?" Daniel asked in a timid voice while shifting his weight in the chair as it seemed to consume him.

"On me, of course. You can leave in the morning, or now if you would like. You'll travel using my jet, stay at my place, and all your expenses while you're there are on my bill. Consider it my treat for putting you in an uncomfortable situation."

"I-I-I don't know, Stuart. It just goes against all of my beliefs, morally and professionally. I just feel that I am part of it by not saying anything. None of this feels right," Daniel replied.

Natalia put on her best little sister act, gave him her sweet, innocent puppy dog eyes, and said, "Come on, Daniel. It will be fun. Our first family vacation."

He looked at her quickly, then immediately away. He wasn't fooled. Not anymore.

Stuart jumped into the rescue, raising his voice, "You'll never find another job if you have a reputation for being a whistleblower. You know that would ruin you."

The threat did the trick when the nice boss and sister acts didn't seem convincing.

"Okay. Tell me what you want me to do," Daniel sighed.

Acting unsurprised, as if this was exactly what he expected, Stuart answered, "My car will pick you up tomorrow morning at 5:00 a.m. to take you to the jet. Pack for a week. Or, don't pack at all and buy what you need when you get there. I don't care. Just meet the car at 5:00 a.m."

Stuart walked over to Daniel's chair and held out his hand. It was an agreement, in addition to his invitation to leave. Daniel stood up with difficulty, straightened out his pants, looked Stuart in the eyes, and shook his hand confidently.

"See you in a week, then."

He walked to the elevator, which was inconveniently unavailable. He stood, basically in the same room as Natalia and Stuart, staring at the elevator doors as if he couldn't turn around after his big exit. The doors finally opened; he stepped on but didn't turn around before the doors closed behind him.

Daniel Webber was going down.

In the tropics

Natalia sat up abruptly as she woke up and forgot where she was. She tried to jump up, but she was buckled into a seat. She looked around frantically, realizing that she was in Stuart's private jet and alone. She was certain Daniel had boarded with her, but her pure exhaustion must have pulled her into a deep sleep the second she sat down. Where was Daniel? Did he get off the plane before takeoff? She only had one thing to do, and that was to get Daniel on the plane. How did she screw that up? She unbuckled her seatbelt rather aggressively, but when she went to stand, she was yanked back down to the seat. Her buckle was stuck in her coat pocket. She frustratedly pulled at the buckle the way you would pull on a car seatbelt that is locked into place. You pull harder and harder and realize the only way to free yourself is to stop and relax, then pull slowly.

Movement at the front of the plane caught her eye as Daniel exited the bathroom and made his way to his seat. Natalia let her head fall back to the seat and closed her eyes as she inhaled deeply, realizing she had been holding her breath since she woke up. She finally lifted her head and looked over as Daniel took his seat. He was smiling and laughing to himself.

"Do you remember when we met after work for drinks at The Cellar, and I walked into the wrong bathroom?" The memory seemed to lighten his spirits and make him chuckle again.

"I'm not sure if I would've noticed if those women hadn't walked in. There was no urinal, but wow, you ladies have stalls for days. We guys are lucky if there's one stall, and if there's a door, it's a bonus. Not to mention, it was so clean. I know we were in a nicer place, but why do these hot, new clubs feel like they have to be so obscure with the bathroom signs? How the hell was I supposed to know that a picture of an old barrel meant it was the ladies' room?"

She was happy to see his smile, even though he was looking out the window. She wanted him to look at her, so she added, "Thank goodness Bunny came in. It sounded like those women were going to kick your ass."

She saw the muscles in his neck tighten, and his smile drop suddenly from his face. The mere mention of Bunny and he was reminded of why they were riding on the private jet.

His face was red and sweaty despite the comfortable, conditioned air on the plane. He sat rigidly upright, grabbed a magazine, and flipped forcefully from one page to the next, not absorbing anything he was looking at. He sighed deeply, like a father who was disappointed by his child.

***

Natalia knew he was mad. He would never look at her the same way. She wanted him to be her partner in crime. She wanted them to understand each other on a deeper level and take on this crazy world together. But, as she watched him open-mouth chew his gum, she realized they were not the same. She would do her best to win him over. She would convince him, one way or another, that Stuart's plan was solid. But then, she decided, she would let him go. He could take his payoff and ride off into the sunset without her, and she would be alone again with no family.

The man, who mere months ago, looked at her as his precious long-lost half-sister, now looked at her with disgust and a bit of fear. She wondered how much he really knew. Sure, he knew Natalia was part of the plan, but did he know how much she was involved? Did he know she was the one who pulled the literal and metaphorical trigger? Did he know how much she enjoyed it? If he knew everything, he would be afraid, so he is either a very good actor or more clueless than he lets on.

***

Awaking her from an unexpected sleep was a deep voice, "Just a heads up, we will be landing in about ten minutes. If you want to look out of your window on the plane's right side, you can see the infamous Widow's Peak. Well, infamous to us pilots anyway." He laughed to himself but still over the intercom. Natalia straightened up, wiping some drool from the side of her mouth, and looked out of the window as the pilot continued, "This runway is famous because both takeoffs and landings approach from the west, with the airplanes heading at very high speeds to a three-hundred-foot cliff. Not to make you nervous, but many planes have met their demise off Widow's Peak." The captain let out another laugh.

Natalia wondered if all pilots found this funny or if his sense of humor was just as dark as hers.

In the distance, Natalia saw the cliff to which he had been referring. It was absolutely beautiful. It reminded her of a commercial or a famous piece of artwork. It was so familiar, and rightly so. Certainly, a place of this beauty must have been painted or photographed thousands of times.

As they crossed the cliff to circle around, Natalia watched the waves crash below against the jagged, sharp rocks.

BYGONES

T he siblings rode to the hotel from the airport in silence, and Natalia was starting to understand what a miserable trip it would be if they couldn't even communicate anymore. But, to her surprise, Daniel cheered up once they had dropped off their things in their room.

"Let's enjoy this. Bygones, right? We don't need to think about what awaits us back at home. For now, let's go have some fun. What do you say?"

This was music to Natalia's ears. She knew there was no such thing as forgive and forget, or bygones, as Daniel put it, but it was refreshing to pretend they were just two siblings on a nice vacation. A week's worth of uncomfortable silence would be unbearable.

"Daniel, that sounds great. Thank you. I'll run to the bathroom quickly, and then we can explore the resort."

Natalia unzipped her bag, pulled out her purse and makeup case, and headed into the bathroom. With all the awkward togetherness, she had almost forgotten to take in the beautiful condo with coastal, Mexican, yet minimalistic decorations—typical Bunny. The bathroom had a large, separate dressing area, a long counter, bright lights, and a magnification mirror. Natalia could not imagine why anyone would ever want to get that close of a look at their face, but she knew Bunny had the same setup back in New York. After using the bathroom, she packed a few essentials in her purse. She stared at her reflection to give herself a silent pep talk. The syringe, the powder, and the drops took up little space, and she was unlikely to need them. But if somehow she was misreading Daniel's intentions, she would rather be safe than sorry. She threw lip gloss, mascara, and a small tube of sunscreen on top of the other things.

When she left the bathroom, she was shocked to find Daniel standing there, waiting in his swimsuit, a loud Hawaiian shirt, and shockingly-white sunscreen on his nose.

"Daniel, you do realize that it is almost sundown, right? We can stop by the pool if you like, but I doubt you will need sun protection."

"I like to practice safe sunning. Plus, it keeps the wrinkles away," Daniel declared while grabbing his towel and moving to open the front door.

"You do you," Natalia said with a little laugh.

Shocked that she used the awful saying but also amazed at how fitting it was to the current situation. She lifted her gaze to see Daniel frozen by the door with his hand on the knob.

"That's what Stuart says," Daniel stated looking down at his feet in disappointment.

"Yeah," Natalia chuckled a bit more to herself. "It's such a dumb saying, though, isn't it?"

No longer in the mood for forgiveness, Daniel, without looking up from the doorknob, said, "I hope you don't mind, but I think I want to head out on my own for a walk." Then, without waiting for an answer, he opened the door and left.

Watching the soft close of the door, Natalia wondered if she had just made things exponentially worse.

A SUNNY DAY

The Eagle has Landed.

Natalia rolled her eyes while typing a reply to Bunny's bizarre text message.

WTF?

Then her phone rang.

"I always wanted to say that or text that in this particular instance," Bunny said in an incredibly cheerful voice, considering what they were all dealing with. "Anyhoo, my sister, Hunny, is all checked into the hotel."

"Hunny? You're Bunny, and your sister's name is Hunny?" Natalia scoffed.

"You don't think Bunny is my real name, do you, dear?" Bunny answered in the sweetest possible *don't be a dumbass* tone. "Look, she only knows what she needs to know. She thinks I'm just setting her up with a great guy so she can live as I do. She knows not to ask questions and to keep him happy."

"Do you feel comfortable bringing someone else into this?"

"Girl! She's my sister. I trust her explicitly. Plus, she got all the looks but none of the brains. Even if I told her everything that was going on, she wouldn't understand it. She would smile and nod." Bunny giggled. "She's pretty and sweet but dumb as rocks."

"Okay, so how should I introduce her to Danny?"

"Don't worry, your pretty little head. She knows what he looks like and is on the lookout for him already. You sit back and let the magic happen."

Natalia disconnected, feeling anything but comfortable with the plan.

She walked back in off the beach and past the pool looking for Daniel. She dialed the room, but there was no answer. The pool was close to empty as the late afternoon chill crept in, so she decided to try the inside bar.

Natalia took a seat at the bar and ordered a tall draft beer, hoping she could do precisely what Bunny instructed and enjoy watching the next part of the plan come to fruition.

Maybe Bunny's scheme would work, and Daniel would be happy. She knew he would never look at her the same way, and upon further retrospection, she realized she really didn't need him in her life. It shouldn't matter if the people you surround yourself with are blood relatives as long as they understand and accept you for who you are. That's what she needed. Letting Daniel go would also free her from the need to pretend to be someone she's not. Not to mention, when he smacked his gum, she could hear the saliva swishing around between his cheeks.

Looking up from her beer, she watched a few minutes of the weather report on the TV on the wall. The weather was delightful. She started to think she should be the one to stay and send Daniel back when she reached back down for her beer.

As she brought the frosted glass to her lips, she caught a reflection in the mirror behind the bar. She saw Daniel and a woman resembling Bunny sitting back to back in separate booths. She fought the urge to spin around and spit out her beer but instead played it cool, put her glass back down on the bar, and leaned over slightly to see if she could make out why they were sitting that way.

After getting the right angle, she saw Daniel sitting comfortably in a booth with a plain but naturally pretty woman she pegged as a local. She leaned back the other way, checking the other woman, whom she assumed was Hunny, and saw she looked very cozy with a guy who looked strikingly similar to Daniel.

Natalia downed her beer and signaled to the bartender to get her another one while she texted Bunny.

Is Hunny Hispanic?

As soon as she hit send, three animated dots appeared, reassuring her that at least Bunny was available to reply.

No, silly. Why do you ask?

She shook her head, took a long sip of her fresh beer, and just as she started to reply, she watched as Hunny and the random guy walked out of the bar with their hands all over each other. She replied simply,

Hunny is either an excellent actress or in love.

She watched the dots and replied before Bunny added: *Just not with Daniel.* The dots stopped, and no reply came.

She heard the abandoned phone ringing from the booth Hunny had just left and decided to briefly join Daniel and meet this mystery woman.

***

Natalia stood, left money on the bar for her drinks, and carried her beer to Daniel's table.

Daniel saw her before she got there and gave her the biggest smile she had seen from him since they arrived. She tried not to flinch when the strong smell of electrical fire blew up her nostrils.

"Natalia. I am so glad you are here," he said surprisingly sincerely. He looked over at the woman across from him and continued. "This is my half-sister, Natalia, who I was telling you about."

Shit, shit, shit, Natalia thought to herself. They had only just arrived, and she had already let him out of her sight long enough for him to meet a woman and tell this stranger about her. She kept her face in a smile while running through all the incriminating evidence he could've been sharing.

"Natalia, this is Sunny," Daniel said with a smitten smile.

"No shit!" Natalia laughed and immediately composed herself after seeing the smiles drop off both faces. "It's just that I was just thinking of..." She had nothing—no explanation at all. She certainly couldn't explain to them that she was plotting with Bunny and her sister Hunny when Sunny showed up. The wordplay was hilarious to her but not something she felt she could share with them. "Oh, forget it. It's so nice to meet you." Fortunately, she dodged a bullet as the couple looked way more into each other than what craziness flowed from Natalia's mouth.

Looking back at Daniel, she said, "I'm starting to feel a migraine coming." She rolled her eyes and held her right hand up to her temple, sighing deeply. "So, I thought I would grab a quick beer, then head upstairs and lie down. You don't mind, do you?" she added, looking back and forth between Daniel and Sunny.

While both gave her pitiful looks of sympathy, Sunny was actually the one to reply in beautiful Latino-accented English, "Oh no. I am so sorry. I can see on your face that you are in very much pain. No offense. I get very bad headaches, too. In fact, I have a prescription back at my house if you feel you need it?"

Quite taken aback, Natalia simply replied, "No, but thank you. I probably just need to rest."

"Well, you go rest. I will take good care of him," Sunny said with a wink.

Natalia walked out of the bar and to the elevator bank in a daze. She suddenly felt like she had been played. Was it really a coincidence that Bunny sent Hunny, and Daniel ended up with Sunny? She started to laugh to herself until she laughed so hard that tears streamed down her face, and she began to hiccup.

The elevator doors opened, and a maid walked off, hugging the wall farthest from Natalia, clearly not interested in riding with a hysterical woman.

Head over Heels

Feeling the need to take a vacation from her vacation was driving Natalia mad. The hotel room was growing smaller every day, and with Daniel spending most of his time with Sunny and Natalia not knowing anyone else, she felt like she was on an island all alone. She felt just as isolated as when she was in Hawaii, making her yearn to stand next to a businessman on his way to work, smelling like vodka, or a punk teenager with headphones on, hocking loogies on the sidewalk.

She had to get out. She threw her hair into a messy bun on top of her head, slipped into her bikini, tossed a lightweight, airy sweater over her shoulders, and grabbed her beach bag, prepacked with a towel, sunscreen, her purse, and a magazine, and hustled out of the room and to the elevator. Listening to the music playing through the hallway walls, she concluded that every Mexican song had the same synthetic background beat. Until now, she thought the hotel was looping the same song, but no. The songs changed, but the boom-ti-ti-boom background remained the same. The wait for the elevator was long, and the ride seemed even longer. She wanted to get out of the hotel and into the open air, so every second seemed to take longer than the last. By the time she reached the first floor, it had become a challenge for her. Would she hear a song before leaving the building that had a different bass line? As she walked out of the lobby, the answer was a clear no.

Natalia stepped out into the sun and stopped. She wanted to take it all in. She wondered how so much peace and quiet felt chaotic to her. Debating between the beach and the pool, she looked back and forth between the two. The beach was packed with families, and she was pretty sure she also saw a chicken. Distant music tickled her ears. She followed the sound around the corner to a little stage that was built into the boardwalk heading toward the beach. Rather than the mariachi music she often heard around the hotel, she recognized the bold and elegant music as Flamenco. A few years ago, she spent a week straight watching an internet mini-series on the origin of Flamenco music and dance in Spain. She watched as the guitar player, barely a man, passionately danced his fingers over the guitar strings with ease. His black hair was just long enough to fall casually over his eyebrows as he bent over and played. He was sitting on a bar stool, his pant hems rolled up to his calves and his bare feet propped up on the lower rungs.

Watching him manipulate the instrument to play the arousing music was deeply sensual. As he strummed the final note, he raised his head to the spattering of applause and locked his bold, blue eyes right on Natalia. When she realized she stood there amidst a clapping crowd with her jaw hung open, she closed her mouth and walked down to the beach.

Walking slowly along the shoreline, Natalia picked up small, round rocks and tossed them out, trying to skip them into the water. Most of the rocks simply plunked into the water in a splash, but after watching one perfect rock skip three times before diving into a wave, she startled at the sound of a voice behind her.

"Are you a professional rock skipper?" the voice asked.

Natalia turned to find the sexy guitar player standing about ten feet behind her. Without his guitar, she could see that his button-down linen shirt was wide open, putting his beautiful, tanned pecs and abs on full display.

"Actually, yes," Natalia replied sarcastically.

"I feel blessed by your presence. My name is Paco."

"Natalia," she said, reaching out to shake his hand, which he took in his and kissed gently, all without breaking eye contact.

"The pleasure is all mine."

"Did you just leave your performance?"

"Yes," he said with a smile. "I saw you and knew I must follow you. But it was also my break time." He laughed. "I only play for another hour. Would you like to meet me in the bar for a drink when I am finished?"

She looked at him closer and noticed that his hair, blowing in the breeze, was actually a bit greasy. His eyes were stunning but way too close together. Plus, now that he was standing in front of her, not up on a barstool on a stage, he was actually a bit shorter than her. Was she petty and judging like her mother, picking out flaws before giving the poor guy a chance? Or was this the "rock-star effect," where even the dullest guy looks crazy hot on a stage? That grungy hair, crazy clothes, and even sweat can be sexy from a distance, but up close are just weird. Or maybe, just maybe, she wasn't looking for a man, for a fling, or even to be courted.

She knew Francisco was back home, and this guy couldn't hold a candle to him.

"Thank you, Paco, but I cannot meet you. Your music was amazing, and I will never forget the way it made me feel."

Understanding that this wasn't just an *I'm busy tonight* kind of rejection, he reached for her hand again, kissing it gently. "Maybe in another life." He let her hand drop, turned, and made his way back to the boardwalk.

Natalia stared out to sea for a few more minutes, watching a pod of dolphins play in the waves. Heading back to the hotel, she took the long way around to avoid the boardwalk where Paco was playing. His music drifted away as she began to hear the repetitive hotel music again. She strutted out to the pool to the rhythm of the music, then she had an idea. After looking around nonchalantly, she popped into a cabana, lowering the tent flaps so they closed behind her. These were for reserved guests only, but Natalia had been watching and never saw anyone questioned. If someone asked her to leave, she would just play dumb. She plopped down on the double-sized, cushioned lounge chair and closed her eyes. It only took a minute for her to realize how hot it could get inside with the flaps down, so she sat up, turned on both of the oscillating fans and opened the refrigerator just in case it was stocked. To Natalia's good fortune, she found at least two dozen single-serving bottles of sparkling wine. She popped one open, grabbed a spare, and returned to the lounge. She had no idea how much these would cost to rent, but it was gorgeous. The fans spun slowly enough to be mesmerizing, and everything looked as if it was just redecorated and never used. The tables held shine, even though they were outside.

The lounge was elegant and inviting. At the peak of the tent hung a beautiful chandelier. Now this was the life for her. Her spatial anxiety was gone, the fans slowly pushed clean, crisp air over her body, and the wine was cold and tingly in her mouth. She closed her eyes, taking in every feeling, every smell, every sound, and felt that she could sit there forever when she heard a noise coming from the cabana next door. Hoping it was just someone stocking the supplies and not a family with loud kids, she decided to give it a minute. Then it hit her... baby powder. The strong, clean, fresh smell of baby powder.

Natalia sat up, deciding to hunt down another cabana because surely where there is baby powder, surely there will be smelly-ass diapers close behind. She was stuffing a few more bottles of wine in her beach bag when she heard Daniel's soft voice.

"I am not sure what I should do."

Natalia quietly sat back down and turned off the fans so she could hear better.

"This is your see-ster and your boss?" asked another voice that she assumed was Sunny by how she pronounced sister.

"Yes. Well, my half-sister. Can you imagine how uncomfortable this is for me? It's bad. Really bad."

"How bad could it really be? I think you may be exaggerating just a bit. No offense," Sunny questioned.

"Trust me. You really don't want to know. I don't want to know. I wish I could go back to not knowing. I am sad that they didn't come out and talk to me, and I had to find out on my own, sort of. But I guess they were protecting me or whatever. I just wish it never happened."

"Are you sure that she is really your sister?"

Natalia sat up, offended, muscles tensing all over her body. She could be accused of a lot of things. A lot of really bad things. But she did not make up the sister part. How dare Sunny suggest such a thing. She fought against her defensive nature, not to get up and bust through the tent and give that woman a piece of her mind... or fist. But, no, it was really important that she heard this. She didn't really expect that Daniel could keep quiet about everything, but she certainly thought he could get through the first week without ratting them out.

"I hadn't thought of that." Daniel paused, then quickly continued, "No, I am sure. It all makes sense." He sighed, and Natalia heard a rustle as if they were maybe moving from a seated position to lying down. "I just felt that everything was great. She was the person I had been waiting for all my life. Now I realize she is not what I thought at all. I wish I could just go away. I don't want to be a rat. I don't want to give up my entire career. But how could I live with myself knowing I had protected them? Rules are rules. Right is right. Wrong is wrong. It's black and white."

His sappy voice was disgusting to Natalia. Was he trying to get sympathy sex, or did he really feel this way? She could hear kissing and rubbing and wondered how much privacy people really assumed they had in these things with just a thin layer of fabric between them and the next couple.

"You're a good man, Daniel. I think you know what you need to do. But don't worry, it wasn't her you were waiting for your whole life." More kissing... gross. "It was me."

Natalia groaned, jumped up, and flung open the tent flaps turning the corner to escape the gag-worthy scene.

Thanks to Francisco, she now knew what it was like to care so much about someone that you want to reveal deep, dark secrets; but he had just met this woman. She was frustrated at the quickness with which he could go from pouty and inconvenienced Daniel to head-over-heels in love, betraying everyone for this stranger. It was also annoying. *Who lets themselves get so emotionally involved with someone while on vacation? Obviously, he* couldn't really be in love, and where the hell did he see it going with her living here?

Daniel was a problem. He was a problem that she hoped she could keep in check. But, now Sunny was a problem too. Natalia kicked off her sandals and walked onto the white sand beach. She had a lot of thinking to do and a lot of planning to do. They were leaving tomorrow, which meant she had better get on figuring everything out.

Like nearly everything else in her life, she thought it would be best if she handled it alone. But this didn't only affect her. How she handled this could also determine Stuart and Bunny's future. It was about time that Natalia trusted the people who had been there for her. She pulled out her cell phone and dialed Bunny's number.

A CHOKED UP GOODBYE

Natalia finally crawled out of bed at 7:00 a.m. though she hadn't slept more than a few minutes at a time all night. Her call the previous night with Stuart made her feel a bit at ease, but she wouldn't feel better until she was back in New York with this whole week behind her. He and Bunny had such a calming effect on her. Amidst all the chaos her current situation brought upon them all, they always seemed to have not just a plan but a backup to the backup plans. Sunny was a bit of a wrench in the spinning gears. With Daniel spending all of his time with his new love, Natalia had little time to talk to him about his thoughts on going to the police or going to the board. She had hoped the vacation would relax him and enable her to talk him out of his ethical leanings.

Even after he met Sunny, Natalia held out hope that maybe he would fall in love and just stay with her. But, after overhearing their conversation at the pool, she was sure of only two things: he was smitten with Sunny, if not in love, and he had not changed his mind.

Most of the night, she paced the room, packing and unpacking and packing again. Other times she debated the necessity of vacations. If there was one thing she learned from having two vacations in a few short months, it was that she didn't need to go anywhere to relax. Sure, it was beautiful, but she could only relax on a lounge chair at the beach for so long. Relaxing was boring. But maybe it just felt that way because she had been doing it alone. Maybe, relaxing on the beach with Bunny, Stuart, and even Francisco would have a different feel. Watching others take walks on the beach, swim in the ocean, and play games in the pool was depressing when all you could do was stare.

After getting dressed, she stuffed her cosmetics bag along with her last few pieces of clothing from last night into her suitcase and did one more sweep of the room for any of her things, or Daniel's, but he hadn't been there since they arrived. She agreed to meet Daniel at the airstrip by 8:00 a.m., but she had one more thing she had to deal with before she left. The concierge had her taxi waiting and helped load her suitcase while she plopped into the back seat.

"Airport, miss?" the driver asked while eyeing her through his rearview mirror.

"Yes, but can you make a quick stop at this address on the way?" she asked as she handed the driver a small piece of paper.

The driver nodded, and Natalia sat back in her seat, thankful that the locals spoke such fluent English.

A few minutes later, the taxi driver pulled into a street of small but well-maintained bungalows. Each house couldn't have been more than three rooms total, but they were quaint, with bright, colorful paint and simple and tasteful landscaping. A hotel van passed them, heading in the other direction, back toward the hotel, and she wondered if all of these people worked there.

That would explain why not one of these cute little houses had a car. The driver pulled up in front of a pink, baby-girl-bedroom-colored house with navy blue trim and door. Of all the adorable places on this street, this one was by far the ugliest. Though every other house looked like they just took whatever leftover paint they had and made it work, this one looks like they had last choice or were color blind. The color was nauseating, plus the fact that every plant and flower was the same pink color—no variety at all.

"Thanks. I'll just be a minute," Natalia called to the driver as she hopped out and jogged up to the blue door with the pink, flowery wreath. She knocked on the door and realized that all of these coordinating flowers were artificial, which somehow made it worse.

Natalia heard the footsteps approaching quickly; then, the door swung open.

Sunny's face initially reflected excitement and surprise but quickly turned to disappointment.

"Oh. Hi," she said quietly. "I thought you were Daniel. I was excited that he came back to me, but it is just you. No offense."

"None taken."

Natalia cringed.

"I am so sorry, but you just missed him. He must not have known you were coming by to get him. He thought you were meeting at the airport."

Natalia smiled and said, "Oh, no. I am here to say goodbye to you."

"Oh, come in, come in." Sunny stepped back, holding the door open.

Natalia stepped in and continued, "You have made Daniel so happy, so I just wanted to bring you a gift before I go."

Sunny stopped and turned around to look at Natalia, blushing. "We are very thankful to have found each other, but you did not need to get me a gift."

"I didn't have a chance to wrap it," Natalia said, pulling a bottle of perfume from her hoodie pocket with one hand and pulling the front by the drawstrings up over her mouth and nose. With Sunny's mouth wide open in surprise, Natalia spritzed the perfume three times rapidly into Sunny's face, then stepped back toward the door.

With her sweatshirt still pulled over her face to filter out the toxins, Natalia still attempted to hold her breath while watching Sunny stumble backward, coughing frantically. Within seconds, Sunny had fallen through her glass coffee table, her face had turned blue, and her coughing—and breathing—had stopped.

Satisfied, she wiped the bottle down and placed it by the windowsill, which was slightly open. With luck, the wind would blow it over, and it would crash to the floor on its own, but either way, she didn't want to take it with her.

Natalia opened the front door, locking it behind her, and yelled back into the house while she pulled it closed, "Goodbye!"

She jogged back to the taxi, jumped into the back seat, and continued to the airport.

THE GUM POPPER

Natalia followed the downtrodden Daniel up the stairs and onto the plane. The private jet was large enough to comfortably transport eight guests in addition to the flight crew, but this flight would just be the two of them. Natalia passed by the bearded pilot in the cockpit and felt increasingly nervous about the flight home. He gave her a reassuring nod and then went back to his preflight checks. Natalia and Daniel each took a seat on opposite sides of the aisle in large captain's chairs that faced decent-sized tables. A decorative basket of individual water and wine bottles, along with snacks, had been set on each of their tables.

Natalia stared at Daniel as he blew his nose loudly into a couple of tissues and then tossed them onto the table. As she watched him sob into his hands, she wondered how much she really knew him. Was he always this fragile? Did she just go on believing he was the brother she had always wanted? His habits were disgusting. Natalia had happily killed for lesser offenses.

Daniel took a deep breath, blew his nose, tossed the tissues onto the table again, and sighed loudly.

Gross! Natalia thought to herself. *Throw your tissues away. There is no need to line them up like a trophy collection.*

She kept an eye on him as he sat back and kicked off his shoes under the now snot-covered table. The strong smell of old, funky cheese and eggs wafted up to her nose. She quickly turned her head toward the window and covertly pulled her sleeve over her nose. Her upper lip curled, and her nostrils flared. Had he always been this disgusting? It wasn't as if they were on a packed commercial flight. Have some manners, for crying out loud. He threw his nasty booger rags on the table, then kicked off his stinky shoes, letting the smell coat the walls of the airplane. How had she missed these gross habits?

Daniel sighed again, which made Natalia turn to face him. If he wanted to say something, why didn't he just say it? Was he waiting for her to prompt him?

"Are you going to be okay?" Natalia asked, not really caring so much as wanting the aggravating sighing to stop.

"I don't know how I ever lived without her, to tell you the truth."

Natalia sat up straight and felt a chill down her spine. Her whole body became stiff, stress filled with frustration. She gritted her teeth and stared at the weak mass of a man.

She reached down to pick up her purse and headed to the toilet.

"I'll be right back," she said to Daniel.

Daniel just nodded, and as she turned her back, she heard him popping his gum in his mouth.

Pop.

Pop.

POP!

She stopped in her place, took a deep breath, smiled through clenched teeth, and walked toward the bathroom at the front of the plane.

Damn, 9-11

Daniel popped a few more pieces of gum in his mouth. Somehow, chewing gum calmed his upset stomach. He thought that maybe he would pour a stiff drink from the liquor cabinet once they took off. This pain was all-encompassing. Nothing would ease the tightening of his chest or the tumbling of his stomach until he was back with Sunny. He couldn't wait for the moment they landed so he could call and book her a flight to come to stay with him. Or he could just settle things back home, resign and head back. Surely Stuart would lend him the jet again just to get rid of him. He would vow to leave Stuart and Natalia's business alone and disappear if only he could live out his days with Sunny.

He looked up, startled as he felt the plane pull away only seconds after hearing the exterior door slam. Natalia was still not back from the bathroom. The private jet probably had very extravagant bathrooms, but he was sure it was safer to be seated and buckled up before takeoff.

Daniel called out to Natalia, "Hey! We are taking off." Feeling stupid knowing she surely felt the plane move.

Unsure about getting up, he hesitated before unbuckling and walking to the bathroom. The plane accelerated, making it harder and harder to stand.

"Natalia, you need to hurry and sit down," Daniel said, knocking on the bathroom door before turning back to his seat. Halfway back, he stopped and turned back to the bathroom. *She is a grown woman who could care for herself, and he should be in his seat. But what if she hit her head? What if she needs girl supplies? Is there no flight attendant?*

Not hearing any reply, he went back and knocked again. No answer. Frustrated that Natalia was now being selfish and putting him in danger, he turned the knob and gently pushed the door open, revealing an empty room.

Daniel backed up frantically. It was a small plane and there weren't many places she could go. He moved toward the pilot's quarters and banged on the door as he felt the jet reach takeoff speed.

"Hey! Natalia is not here. Stop! We need to go back."

He banged and banged, but the door was locked from the inside, and the engines were so loud he couldn't tell if anyone was answering.

"Damn, 9-11 rules. I'm on a freaking private jet and can't even talk to the pilots," he said as he stumbled back to his seat.

He sat down and rapidly buckled up, knowing when they were airborne, someone would be out to check on him.

Watching the Wreckage

From inside the terminal, crowds gathered, pressed against the window as the fancy private jet picked up speed but never rose off the ground. The plane moved faster and faster until it reached the end of the runway and plummeted at an extremely high speed off the edge of Widow's Cliff.

Airport employees were running every which way, making calls, and sounding alarms, yet trying to stay composed and professional. Firetrucks and ambulances rushed out to the cliff only to stand on the edge and stare at the wreckage.

The plane must have caught fire because out in the distance, the beautiful horizon was accented with bright red flames occasionally licking up above the cliff top. An airplane's fuselage was likely to burn longer at takeoff than landing due to supply.

Natalia watched the chaos and embraced the beauty of the scene. She had done the right thing. She worked so hard to be what he wanted her to be, but in reality, she wanted to be nothing like him, a weak rule follower with more than a handful of disgusting habits. She smiled and felt the tightness that had taken over her body simply release when she stepped off the plane. She looked to her left to see Bunny. With her, as always, was Stuart, looking sharp, though extremely sweaty, dressed as a pilot with his arm over Bunny's shoulder, staring at the unfolding scene. Stuart had not told Natalia his plan for getting off the plane, unseen before it took off, nor did she want to ask. However, he did it; she knew it couldn't have been easy, but it likely had something to do with a hacked autopilot system. Like everything else over the last year, the Vladigans sacrificed so very much for her. Yet, as they looked at her, she knew they did it without question and would do it again.

Stuart walked behind the two women, peeled off his stick-on beard, and gently placed his arms around them. Friends who were closer than family. The three shared a stoic moment staring at the bellowing smoke on the horizon. Stuart's somber grin turned up slightly at the edges as the irony of the situation sank in. One of the first assignments Stuart tasked Daniel with was to bolster the company's Risk Management Plan. Daniel had built an iron-clad insurance policy on the company's aging private jet, which, due to never-ending repairs, had turned into a money pit in recent years. The insurance windfall on the accident would be more positive financial news for MBI.

With slight pressure on their outer shoulders, he turned the women around, and the group walked in silence toward the exit of the terminal.

New Retirement

Natalia had her eyes closed. She was relaxed and comfortable for the first time in as long as she could remember. She listened to the water shuffling shells along the tideline. The seagulls squawked in the distance, making a sound that would be infuriating if not for it being associated with the sea. She opened her eyes behind her oversized sunglasses to a bright, bold blue sky, only broken by the warm and comforting sun. The temperature was a perfect eighty-six degrees with no humidity. She watched as waves lapped upon the shore in a slow yet constant pattern that would put one to sleep if they stared too long. The beach was near empty of people, with a couple of exceptions, including a very tall man walking the shoreline in a thong swimsuit with a large snake around his neck. Natalia sat on a lounge chair under a preppy, striped umbrella staring out toward the ocean and the beautiful, tanned, topless woman walking toward her.

"I know you don't want to talk about it," Stuart said from behind her chair, handing her a cocktail in a pineapple with a little pink umbrella sticking out. "But I didn't think you would go through with it." He settled into the lounge two seats over but kept his eyes on Natalia.

"He just seemed so... broken. My whole life, I imagined what my brother or sister would be like if I had one. Daniel looked just like I always thought he would, but in my imagination, he was strong enough to stand up for himself and me. He would be funny and kind and smart."

"You thought he would be like you," Stuart said as Bunny sat her slightly sandy ass between them.

"I guess I did. I wanted him to understand me, accept me... but I know now that would never happen." Natalia took a sip, closed her eyes, slipped off her glasses, and leaned back on her chair to soak up the warm rays. She was not one to second guess her decisions, and she wouldn't start now.

"In the end, my bitch of a mom was right," she said without opening her eyes or looking at either Bunny or Stuart. "I don't need anyone in my life who doesn't understand me."

"You do you," Stuart said with a wink.

***

They stayed in the Mexican resort a bit longer than they had planned, hoping to avoid the journalists back in New York, along with calls about Daniel's demise. Natalia was surprised that the plane crash was front page news, but there was no mention of a local resort worker going missing, having an accident or being murdered. Their remaining days were filled with relaxation on the beach, by the pool, or in the resort spa, but not one of them mentioned Daniel or anything about their life back in New York. Very few full conversations took place, except for the group vowing to return to the beautiful vacation destination with Francisco for a more extended vacation.

THE UNEXPECTED

Diambu drove them home from the airport. The three rode in silence as if holding their breath, unsure of how everything would play out now that they were back. The city looked different. It felt like the world carried on without them while they were gone. It obviously did, but to know that was to know your insignificance in the world, which caused even more reflection.

Diambu opened the door for them, and while the doormen helped unload their luggage, Natalia turned to Diambu and hugged him. Well, as much of a bear hug that someone half the other person's size can give. He was a tether to the world they left and a sign that she could still exist.

Natalia caught up to the others by the elevator bank. She gave a warm hug to Bunny and a head nod to Stuart as he handed her the newspaper. The couple departed from the lobby to their condo in the private elevator. With Daniel gone, Natalia decided to go straight to her place—she would get her things from Bunny's later. As she waited for her elevator to arrive, she wondered what life would be like now. While away, they didn't talk about what was next regarding her job. All she knew was that she was happy she had found her tribe. She had people who loved her for who she was in all of her odd ways.

The thought of Francisco crossed her mind, and her belly filled with butterflies. She smiled and lifted the newspaper to cover her embarrassingly giddy smile.

The front page blasted a huge headline that immediately caught her eye.

MBI UNEXPECTED GAINS

Following an audit of MBI's pension program, it has been deter-mined that recently retired Chief Financial Officer Ernest Johnson grossly overbudgeted the amount of money necessary for the MBI retirees receiving a pension. The budget adjustment has resulted in an unexpect-ed and substantial gain for the powerhouse company and yet another feather in the cap of CEO Stuart Vladigan.

A yellow piece of sticky tape caught her eye, and though what she was reading was undoubtedly informative, she opened the newspaper to the page Stuart had marked and read the article.

TRAGEDY IN THE TROPICS

MBI's Chief Financial Officer, Daniel Webber, is one of two people believed to have perished in the plane crash off the coast of Mexico. Mr. Webber was traveling back from a vacation with close friend and men-tor Stuart Vladigan, his wife, Bunny Vladigan, and Daniel's sister. Mr. Webber was scheduled to fly out on Mr. Vladigan's private jet a few days before the rest of his party, but the ill-fated flight barely made its way off the runway. Due to the nature and location of the wreck, authorities report it could be months before they can salvage the wreckage with hopes of finding the cause. Although no bodies have been recovered, the flight manifest identifies the other victim as pilot Captain Dick Hertz from White Plains, New York.

With Natalia having left Mr. Hertz's dead body at the bottom of the Hudson River weeks ago and the official investigation unlikely to retrieve the wreckage, Stuart's plan was executed brilliantly, and no one was the wiser.

***

The elevator arrived, and she stepped in and to the side, trying to make way for the sweet, old woman getting off.

"Oh, I'm not getting off here," the old woman said in a shaky, high-pitched voice.

"Oh, okay," Natalia replied, a bit confused.

"I am heading out to take my dogs for a walk. But look at me." She laughed hysterically. "I forgot my dogs." She continued to laugh so hard that she was crying.

Natalia chuckled as the woman let out a long, post-laugh sigh.

"You sure do look cheery today," the woman said with a smile, wiping away the tears.

Natalia internally scolded herself for not remembering that she should be mourning the loss of her half-brother.

"I think I am just ready for a fresh start."

"New beginnings are good, aren't they?" she said as the elevator reached her floor.

"Would you like me to hold the elevator while you get your dogs?" Natalia asked.

"Oh, you sweet girl. Thanks, but it may take me a while. I'll catch the next one." She stepped off and turned around. "Not everyone is so kind to the elderly. Thank you." And the doors closed on the most ironic statement Natalia had ever heard.

A few floors later, Natalia stepped off the elevator and unlocked the door to Daniel's condo... her condo. It hadn't crossed her mind what she would do with his things. She would ask Bunny and Stuart if they knew where she could donate them. Maybe the owners would let her stay or even better she could buy the place and redecorate, she thought as she looked around the room.

Leaving her brand new bags purchased in Mexico by the door, she walked into the kitchen to grab a drink of water. She grabbed a glass from the cabinet and on her way to the water cooler she spied a piece of paper on the counter containing a list. She stopped to read it. Her eyes grew wider and filled with tears as she took in each pro and con and finally glanced back up to the question at the top of the page...

SHOULD I SHARE WHAT I KNOW ABOUT NATALIA AND STUART'S LOVE AFFAIR?

Her stomach clenched as her last couple of weeks of conversations with Daniel ran through her mind like a film being fast-forwarded, and as if in slow motion, her glass fell from her hand and crashed to the floor.

With tears in her eyes, she glanced at the final bullet point under the CON list. Written in bold red letters and underlined, it read:

5. SHE'S MY SISTER

After months of her hiding her disappointment at his insistence to call her his half-sister, he may have changed his tune.

Natalia became enveloped in the noxious smell of sulfur. It was the first time she had associated that odor with an emotion. She hated the smell and pinched her nose to no avail. The smell was not coming from the room. It was coming from her. It was the strong smell of remorse.

With her eyes watering from emotion and the smell, Natalia was temporarily distracted as her phone vibrated on the counter.

It was Bunny sharing another contact.

Thank You For Reading

If you enjoyed MAKING A KILLING, please consider leaving an honest review on your preferred platform.

Your feedback is invaluable and helps other readers discover new books and authors.

***

If you didn't love it... sorry it wasn't your jam.

Thanks for giving me a try.

want more?

Left **Without Answers** by Cori Nevruz plunges readers into a heart-stopping journey of grief, mystery, and unyielding determination. After the sudden and unexplained loss of her son Hank, Alice is consumed by a relentless need for answers. The vibrant spirit of her boy couldn't just vanish without a trace—there must be more to the story.

As Alice reaches out to Hank's best friend Arnold, she's met with a chilling resistance. Arnold, like everyone else, insists she move on, urging her to let the past rest. But Alice's motherly intuition is a force that cannot be silenced, especially when she begins finding cryptic notes from Hank. Could Hank be reaching out from beyond, or is something more sinister at play?

Alice's quest leads her deep into Hank's hidden life, unraveling a web of betrayal, bullying, and secrets darker than she ever imagined. Each revelation threatens to tip her over the edge of sanity, as she battles the terrifying truths lurking in the shadows.

In a race against time and her own fears, Alice must uncover the truth behind her son's death. But as the specters of Hank's final moments haunt her, Alice faces a chilling realization—some secrets are meant to stay buried. Will her search for answers bring justice, or will it plunge her into a nightmare from which there is no escape?

Left Without Answers is a gripping, suspense-filled thriller that will keep you on the edge of your seat until the final page.

***

Dirty Laundry by Cori Nevruz invites readers into the fragile world of Samantha, a former perfectionist whose once-orderly life spirals into chaos with the addition of a husband and children. As the facade of her perfect suburban existence cracks, Samantha's insecurities deepen, fueled by her husband's relentless criticism and impossible expectations.

Beneath the surface of cheerful smiles and staged social appearances lies a woman teetering on the edge, her hidden turmoil spilling into the pages of a secret journal. But when Samantha confides in a new friend, her carefully constructed life unravels, exposing dangerous truths that threaten both their lives.

What dark secrets could shatter the illusion of Samantha's seemingly perfect life? **Dirty Laundry** is a fast-paced, suspenseful journey into the mind of a mom on the edge.

ABOUT THE AUTHOR

Cori Nevruz

Cori Nevruz is a suspense and thriller author known for her gripping narratives and psychological depth. She has penned three acclaimed novels: <u>Dirty Laundry</u>, a fast-paced thriller that delves into the unraveling mind of a mom pushed to her limits; <u>Left Without Answers</u>, which follows a mother teetering on the edge of madness in her quest for justice; and <u>Making a Killing</u>, a chilling tale of a lethal assassin targeting retired pensioners.

Cori resides in Wilmington, NC, where she balances her writing career with family life alongside her husband and three sons. When she's not crafting thrilling stories, she enjoys reading and passionately following her favorite sports.

For more information, including social media links and contact information, please visit her website at http://CoriWroteABook.com.